The Designer of His Own Fortune

A Have Body, Will Guard Adventure by

Neil S. Plakcy

Copyright 2024 Neil S. Plakcy. This book is a work of fiction. Names, characters, places, and incidents either are products of the author's imagination or are used fictitiously. Any resemblance to actual events or locales or persons, living or dead, is entirely coincidental.

All rights reserved, including the right of reproduction in whole or in part in any form.

Persian proverb: Ezzat-e har kas be-dast-e ân kas ast.

English equivalent: Every man is the smith of his own fortune.

Chapter 1

Cousin Eddie

Aidan

Aidan Greene had just put the eggplant parmigiana casserole in the oven when his husband Liam's cell phone rang. He stuck the phone under his chin as he opened the refrigerator to pull out a bottle of Côtes de Provence rosé wine to serve with dinner.

He didn't recognize the number, so he answered formally. "Good afternoon. This is Aidan Greene of Agence de Securité. How may I help you?"

"I'm trying to reach my cousin Billy," the man said.

Aidan's first reaction was that the call had to be from one of Liam's Navy buddies, because he hadn't answered to Billy since he left the military and came out of the closet. But then the word 'cousin' registered.

"You mean Liam McCullough," he said. "Who's calling, please?"

"Oh, that's right, Aunt Doris said he changed his name. To something stupid, she said. Oh, I don't think it's a stupid name, sorry, I shouldn't have said that."

Aunt Doris, Aidan thought. That comment sounded like it had come out of his mother-in-law's mouth. Not that she considered Aidan her son-in-law—gay marriage didn't fit into her world view.

The man kept talking. "My name is Edwin Gallagher and someone murdered my husband last week. I'm afraid they're coming after me next and I need Billy – or Liam – to help me."

Aidan took down his number, which he recognized was one from the US. "Where are you now, Mr. Gallagher?"

"Now? I'm in in my living room."

"Sorry, I meant time zone. We're on the French Riviera, outside Nice. I presume you don't want Liam to call you in the middle of the night."

"It doesn't matter. I'm not sleeping. But I'm in Florida, Boca Raton. That's north of Miami."

"I'll have Liam call you as soon as he gets in," Aidan said.

"Thank you. I'm so glad I reached you. Aunt Doris said Billy travels a lot for his work. Are you his assistant?"

"I'm his husband, and business partner."

"Thank you again, Mr. Greene. I really hope you can help me."

"We'll see what we can do," Aidan said.

Aunt Doris. Liam had never spoken much about cousins, so he had no way to place Edwin Gallagher in the scheme of his family. But he could try.

Liam was in the shower, so he grabbed his laptop computer, nearly stumbling over their little lion-faced dog Hayam sunning herself on the floor. He didn't blame her; January had dawned cold and rainy and for the last two weeks they had been suffering through a mistral, a bitter wind that swept through the valleys of the Rhône and the Durance Rivers to the coast of the Mediterranean.

Hayam had come into Aidan's life in Tunisia, and she was definitely a warm-weather dog.

He logged onto the internet and searched for Edwin Gallagher of Boca Raton, hoping to discover his husband's name and the record of his death. He was surprised at how quickly the result came up. Darius Ashoori, 65, of Boca Raton, Florida had been shot in his Jaguar after a shopping trip to the Boca Town Center mall.

Police believed Mr. Ashoori had been targeted because of his expensive jewelry and the shopping bags he carried from Louis Vuitton, Gucci, and Versace. He had been on his way home and stopped at a liquor store, where he was accosted and shot. He was survived by his husband, Edwin Gallagher.

"I thought you were fixing dinner," Liam said, as he came into the living room. Naked, of course, drying his hair with a towel. Aidan was momentarily distracted from his search by the magnificence of his husband's body.

Even at forty years old, Liam looked almost as good as he had the day he left the US Navy SEALs. Broad shoulders, beefy pecs and biceps, tapering down to a narrow waist. His ample cock was at what he called parade rest, hanging limply in a thick nest of dark blond pubic hair. His legs were ropy and muscular.

"Eyes back in your head," Liam said. "Dinner?"

"Put the towel around your waist if you don't want me to look."

"You can do more than look," he said, as his trouser snake began rearing up to strike. He walked over close to Aidan and Aidan's mouth watered, and not from the smell of eggplant.

"We don't have much time before dinner's ready," Aidan said. "Bring it on, buddy."

Liam positioned himself so that Aidan could suck him where he stood, his legs spread. Aidan tongued his slit, licked up the stalk, then took the whole thing in his mouth. Liam put his hands in Aidan's hair as he sucked up and down, using a quick vacuum motion intended to get his husband off as soon as possible.

Aidan stuck his right index finger in his mouth, wet it well, then reached behind Liam and poked it up his ass. Liam jerked for a moment and then moaned in pleasure.

It didn't take long. Either Aidan was a much better cocksucker than he thought, or Liam had been playing with himself in the shower. He came in a brief spurt, and Aidan swallowed it. As he leaned back and wiped his mouth, he said, "You primed that pump, didn't you?"

"Why do you think I walked out here bare-ass naked?"

"Because you're a big exhibitionist," Aidan said. "You wouldn't even mind if someone came to the door while we were busy."

"Sure I would. I don't like it when you get distracted."

"Idiot. Go get dressed and I'll finish getting dinner ready."

Aidan had the table set by the time Liam came back out, this time in a pair of khaki shorts and a polo shirt that accentuated his muscles.

Aidan poured them both glasses of the rosé and Liam leaned back against the tile counter as Aidan threw together a salad. Miniature heirloom purple, yellow, and red tomatoes with butter lettuce from the greenhouse next door. Artichoke hearts and black olives went in along with shredded carrots, tiny cubes of cheese and croutons Aidan made from stale bread.

Hayam joined them, but she smelled only vegetables, so she retreated to her plush bed in the corner.

As Aidan worked, he said, "You got an interesting phone call while you were in the shower. You have a cousin named Edwin Gallagher in Boca Raton, Florida?"

Liam frowned. "Edwin? You sure?"

"He called your mother Aunt Doris."

"Must be from her side," he said. "Gallagher was her maiden name. Oh wait, Eddie. He was about ten years older than me, and my mother didn't talk to her brother that much, so I've only seen him a couple of times in my life. Why in the world did he call me?"

"Because his husband was murdered and he thinks he's next."

Chapter 2

Label Queen

Liam

Liam kept trying to remember cousin Eddie. According to Aidan, he had a dead husband, which meant he was gay. But try as he might, he couldn't remember more about him than a skinny guy in his twenties when Liam was a teenager.

They'd had one conversation, as he recalled. Eddie was curious as to why he was going into the Navy rather than college. He remembered Eddie being squeamish about basic training. But that was it.

When the salad was finished, Aidan put it in the refrigerator and the two of them sat in the living room, the scent of the bubbling casseroles wafting from the kitchen. "You need to call this guy back," Aidan said. "He's your family."

"Barely. You know anything more?"

Aidan showed him the computer screen. "Sounds like a snatch and grab," Liam said. "Why would Eddie think someone's after him?"

"I don't know. That's why you need to call him."

"You know how I feel about my family."

"There are two kinds of family for gay men. Birth family and found family. Cousin Eddie seems to span both. And you have never stood down when someone gay needs our help." Aidan smiled. "Especially someone who can pay."

"Do we know that he can?"

Aidan hit a couple of keys. "According to this real estate price site, he lives in a two-million-dollar house. The *Wall Street Journal* says that Ashoori was a fashion designer in New York who sold his company to a conglomerate for twenty million." He looked up from the screen. "I'd say your cousin can afford to pay us."

The timer rang on the oven, and they moved to the kitchen table. Aidan sliced portions of the casserole and served it along with garlic bread. "Good thing we got business taken care of earlier," Liam said. "Wouldn't want garlic breath on my junk."

"Just because you finished doesn't mean I did," Aidan said.

"The eggplant is delicious," Liam said. "Everything home grown?"

Aidan frowned at the change of subject, but said, "The artichokes come from a jar, and the olives from the market. Everything else from the greenhouse."

During the Covid isolation, their neighbors Slava and Thierry had built a greenhouse and with the help of young friends begun growing much of the fruit and vegetables they ate.

"We're getting spoiled by all this fresh food in the winter," Liam said.

"Prepare to be spoiled further. Thierry baked a chocolate cake, which they're bringing over for dessert."

"Extra laps on my run tomorrow morning."

"That is, if we're still here. We might be on our way to sunny Florida."

"What did you think of cousin Eddie?" Liam asked.

"Hard to get much of a read from a brief conversation. He's upset, not sleeping. But that could be grief rather than fear."

"After we eat see what else you can dig up on his husband before we call him back."

"Are you worried about seeing your mother?" Aidan asked. "Isn't she still in New Jersey?"

"I wouldn't know. Haven't spoken to her since last month, and all I did was wish her a Merry Christmas and a Happy New Year, and ask about my sisters."

"I doubt we'll run into her then," Aidan said.

They finished the eggplant parmigiana, and followed it up with salad. When their plates were clean, Liam said, "I'll do the dishes and you do the computer."

Aidan moved back to the living room, and when Liam joined him, he said, "I didn't find much. If we take the job we'll have to get Richard to pull a profile."

Richard was a British hacker they used regularly to find information and circumvent online regulations. They didn't ask what laws he broke to help them, and he didn't volunteer anything. Liam liked it that way. "All I found were photos of Darius's creations and a few articles about his business."

They looked at the pictures together and then back at the police report. "Gucci and Versace. What a label queen," Liam said.

"The police report doesn't say what was stolen," Aidan said. "This happened to some cousins of my mother's years ago, in Miami. The husband was flashing a gold Rolex at a shopping mall and someone followed them back to their rental, which didn't have security. Thieves prey on old people over there."

"He was only sixty-five," Liam said. "Not that old."

"Said the man who's obsessing about turning fifty this year."

"Eddie's only about five years older than I am. So he was this guy's boy toy."

Hayam jumped up and began barking. "Speaking of the elderly," Liam said.

Aidan knocked him on the shoulder. "Be nice to the guests."

Aidan opened the door to their next-door-neighbor Thierry, who held a huge chocolate cake. His husband Slava stood behind him. They were in their sixties, and it was a later-in-life love affair for both.

"You're killing us with these desserts," Liam said.

Thierry handed the cake to Aidan and waved his hand. "We'll give the leftovers to the boys. They work hard in the garden."

Aidan sliced the cake and they sat around the kitchen table again. "What is new?" Slava asked.

"We may have a case that requires travel," Aidan said. "A cousin of Liam's in the United States."

"I haven't decided if we're taking the case or not," Liam said.

"But you have not worked for a while, have you?" Slava asked.

The cake was three layers tall, with a hazelnut puree between the bottom and the middle, and a rich chocolate ganache between the middle and the top. Everyone groaned with pleasure as they finished their slices.

"We were very busy in the month before Christmas," Aidan said. "Lots of foreign shoppers who wanted close protection. Nothing since the new year. And the weather hasn't helped. Why come to the Côte d'Azur during the mistral? At least Liam's cousin lives in Florida, where it will be warm."

"And you will want us to look after the petite Hayam," Thierry said. "What a pleasure for us! We are still hoping that we may be grandfathers someday, but Arseny and Giovanni are busy with their lives. So Hayam will have to do."

He turned to Aidan and said, "And what about you and Liam? Will you ever have children?"

"I have learned over the years to never say never to anything," Aidan said. "But I don't think it would be fair to a child, or children, to have fathers who travel often and put themselves into danger. With Hayam, we know that she will miss us, and be well taken care of while we are gone, and then happy to see us again."

They'd finished by then, so he took the plates into the kitchen, followed by Thierry. "How would a child feel, knowing that we might not come back at all? And would we be able to devote ourselves to a client, or worry about saving ourselves for our child?"

"But you will not do this work forever," Thierry said. From the living room, they heard Slava's loud, raucous laughter. "You may retire, as Slava and I have done."

Aidan shook his head. "You haven't retired, either of you. Slava talks to Rafi every day about the spice business, and you are always in the fields with Ekram. I could become a teacher again, I suppose, but I would miss the excitement of working with Liam and the reward that comes from bringing a client to safety."

"I understand that."

"And Liam is a soldier. It's all he has ever known and all

he wants to be. We tried to change, you know. That security business we began with Louis and Hassan. Liam hated every minute of it."

"Then we shall enjoy Hayam," Thierry said.

After Slava and Thierry went home, taking the leftover cake with them, Liam sighed. "What time is it in Florida?"

"It's about nine o'clock here, which makes it four o'clock there," Aidan said.

"Then let's call cousin Eddie and see what's up."

"Edwin," Aidan said. "You want him to call you Liam, you have to call him Edwin.'

Aidan picked up Liam's cell phone and called the number Eddie had used earlier that day. He tried to hand the phone to Liam but his husband refused. "You talk to him first."

Aidan put the phone on speaker and set it down between them.

The voice that answered was rough, a lot of cigarettes and tears behind it. "Hello? Is this Billy?"

"It's Aidan. We spoke earlier today. Liam is on speaker with me."

"Thank God you called me back. I've been beside myself."

"Let's start with what happened to your husband."

"It was an ordinary day. He wanted to go shopping at the mall but the weather was nice and I wanted to work in the garden." He began to cry. "If I'd gone with him."

"If you'd gone with him, you might be dead, too," Aidan said. "I read the police report online. He carried shopping bags from expensive stores out of the mall, is that correct?"

"Yes. God forbid he should buy anything at less than full price. And he'd have allergic fits if he got next to anyone wearing clothes from JC Penney. He'd recognize that little fox logo and start to sneeze."

"Sounds like a winner," Liam muttered under his breath. Aidan waved his hand at him.

"And then he stopped at a liquor store? Was it in a bad neighborhood?"

Edwin Gallagher laughed harshly. "There are no bad neighborhoods in Boca Raton," he said. "No, it's one of those big-box liquor and wine stores. Beer, Wine and More. The police think that Darius was followed from the mall because he was rich. But if they killed him for his money, why didn't they take his gold jewelry? Or any of the bags from the car? Or the Rolls Royce, for that matter?"

"Maybe they were frightened off," Liam said.

"Billy, is that you?"

"I go by Liam now, Eddie."

"I understand. Nobody has called me Eddie since I was a boy."

"So, Edwin," Liam said. "What did the police tell you about the actual shooting?'

Edwin gulped. "He got out of the car. He hadn't even locked the door when another car pulled up beside him. They shot him twice, in the head. Then they drove away."

He began crying again, and they waited until he caught his breath. "I'm sorry. It's still so raw. There were two witnesses an aisle away, a pair of Boca Babes. They couldn't tell the make or model of the car. Just that it was some kind of American or Japanese sedan."

Edwin paused. "Typical Boca Babes. If it's not a Porsche or a Lamborghini they don't recognize it."

"That's all?" Liam asked.

"They called 911 and the police came, but Darius was

already dead. The detective told me there was nothing anyone could have done."

"Was Darius involved in anything illegal?" Liam asked. "That double-tap to the head sounds like a professional hit."

"That's why I'm worried," Edwin said, which triggered another round of tears. It took him a moment to calm down. "I grew up reading the New York *Post*, and I kept reading as an adult. I loved all the true crime stories. I know Darius was involved in some shady business in New York, but I thought he'd put that all behind him when he retired."

He paused. "Although."

Liam waited for Edwin to continue but finally asked, "Although what?"

"He was being secretive lately. Taking phone calls outside where I couldn't hear. Worrying about someone following us on our way home from dinner. At the time, none of it mattered to me, but now I can't stop thinking about those things."

"What do the police think?"

"There have been a rash of shootings at the mall. They think it's an organized gang but they don't have any leads." He took a deep breath. "And then someone tried to break into the house while I was at the police station."

"What happened? Was anything stolen?" Liam asked.

"The detective followed me home, but by the time we got there the burglars had been chased away. They broke the glass in the back door, but that triggered the alarm, and they didn't get inside. The detective said she thinks it was a result of Darius's death being in the newspapers, but I think it's more, and I'm very frightened. I had a company put shatterproof glass back there, but I don't even feel safe in my own home."

Liam looked at Aidan, who stared back at him.

"Please, Liam?" Edwin said. "I can pay you whatever you charge. I just... we don't have any children, or relatives we're close to, and our friends are all busy living their lives. I don't have anyone here I can feel safe with."

"Have you told the police about your suspicions?"

"They'll think I'm a nervous old queen. And what can I say to them, really? Darius always kept a few secrets from me. The occasional restroom activity in New York. How much his diamond watch really cost. I didn't care. But maybe I should have."

Liam sighed. Edwin had some reason to be worried, and Aidan was right, he couldn't step away from someone in trouble. "We'll have a contract sent to you, and if you agree to the terms, we'll get there as soon as we can."

Aidan took over. "We work through an agency here in France which covers us for liability and so on, so we need to send you an agreement to cover our expenses and the cost of our time."

He quoted Edwin a figure assuming they'd be there for a week. "Of course, if we stay longer, you'd have to keep paying our daily rate."

"That's no problem. Can you email me the agreement? And how soon after I sign can you get here?"

Aidan took down Edwin's email address. "I'll get the form out to you in the next few minutes. The Agence de Securité will require a thousand-dollar down payment on a credit card. Once that comes through, we'll book our flights."

"Thank you. You may think I'm over-reacting, but I really believe having some protection could be the difference between life and death for me."

Chapter 3

Perfect Target

Aidan

"I'm glad you made that decision," Aidan said, after they had ended the call. Liam remained on the sofa while Aidan moved over to the desk and opened his laptop. "The man's your family, and it's obvious he has the money to pay us. I don't have it in me to turn him down."

With Hayam curled beside his feet, locking him in place, Aidan pulled up their standard contract with the Agence. He edited it to provide the right details and emailed it to the address Edwin had given him.

While he waited to get the signed contract back, he researched flights from Nice to Florida. After making several adjustments to his search terms, he found the best way. He pushed his chair back, disturbing the dog, who snorted once and walked across the wooden floor to grab a plastic bone and begin chewing it.

"I've got some flights picked out," he said to Liam, who looked up from the sofa. "The best way to go is to fly non-stop from Paris to Miami via Air France. It leaves at 1:20 PM and gets in at 5:30 PM. It's a ten-hour flight, but at least it's direct."

"But we're not in Paris," Liam said. He had his reading glasses perched on his nose, which Aidan found adorable.

"That's not a problem. We can leave tomorrow morning on a 7:30 AM flight and get to Paris at 9:10. Then we have a few hours to kill at Roissy. The later flight gets in at 12:20 and that's not enough time to make an international connection."

Aidan looked back at his screen. A new message had popped in, which had the signed contract attached to it. "We have the contract," he said to Liam.

"Then I guess we're going to Florida."

Aidan picked up his cell phone and dialed the number again. "Edwin, it's Aidan. We can come to Florida and look after you until we figure out what's going on. We'll be on a flight tomorrow morning from Nice which gets us into Miami at 5:30 in the evening."

"Just in time for rush hour," Edwin said. "But by the time you get your bags and get through Customs, you'll have missed some of the traffic."

Aidan ended the call, and Liam stood. "I'll get to work on the electronics. You can start packing."

As Aidan threw a load of laundry into the washer, Liam began putting together things that needed to be charged, from their tiny high-beam flashlights to Aidan's Kindle. While the washer ran, Aidan chose the clothes they'd need. They shared shirts and cargo shorts, with multiple pockets for phones, flashlights, pocketknives, and other necessary tools of their trade. Liam's legs were longer so he needed his own slacks. They each had preferred underwear styles—jockstraps for Liam, boxers for Aidan.

The community where Edwin lived had a pool and a gym, so Aidan added workout gear and swimsuits. By then, an email had come in with a note that the deposit Edwin had sent to the Agence's PayPal account was being processed. Aidan made the airline reservations and booked them a rental car at the Miami airport. He texted Slava to ask for a ride to the airport the next morning, and received a thumbs-up in return.

It was already late, but there was still a lot of work to be done. Liam inventoried spare batteries and extra jump drives and photo cards. He made sure their iPhones, iPads and laptops had been updated to the latest software versions and checked their walkie-talkies. Since they were going to a foreign country, he left their weapons and bullets stored in the gun safe in the office.

They had a standard routine for packing their suitcases, one that Aidan had learned from Liam. Everything went in the same place each time, so that in a hurry, or in the dark, they could find what they needed.

An hour or more passed quickly as they worked in sync, organizing and packing. The laundry moved from the washer to the dryer, and Hayam was sent out to the back yard for her final visit.

At last they were in bed together, Hayam on the floor beside Aidan. She loved both her daddies, but Aidan was the one who had rescued her from the streets of Tunis. And she knew he was the softer touch of the two of them.

"You really don't remember this cousin?" Aidan asked, after he turned the lights off.

Liam yawned. "I've been thinking. He was years older than I was, so he wasn't around much on the rare occasions when Doris took us to visit her brother. And now that I look back, there was an economic thing going on. Uncle Joel and Aunt Ruth were very wealthy and we weren't. I don't think Doris liked having that shoved in her face."

"That can be tough." Aidan turned to face Liam, but his

husband was already asleep, a skill that Aidan envied. Liam had the ability to fall asleep almost immediately, something he'd learned in the Navy. Aidan stared at him for a couple of minutes, until he yawned and turned on his side. The alarm would go off too early in the morning.

When he woke, he wanted to lie there and enjoy the comfort of his own bed, something he'd miss. He'd recently learned the Scottish called that hurkle-durkle, and when they weren't working he loved doing it. But Liam rose and headed for the bathroom, and Aidan knew he had to get up.

After following Liam into the shower, he packed up Hayam's food and toys and walked the dog next door, where Thierry and Slava would be happy to spoil her while Aidan and Liam were gone.

Then Slava pulled his Mercedes sedan into their driveway and they loaded his trunk. The Russian chauffeured them to the airport in Nice with his customary speed and disregard for all driving regulations. "Slava, we'd rather not die before we even start the trip," Aidan said from the back seat, as their neighbor and one-time client zipped around a slow-moving Smart car, which to Aidan resembled a hedgehog rather than a vehicle.

"No worries," Slava said, darting neatly back into traffic as a big truck approached them in the other lane.

Aidan settled for gripping the door handle and kept his mouth shut the rest of the way. The flight to Paris was domestic so they didn't have to go through Customs, and they were on the plane in plenty of time.

"Were you able to dig up much on Edwin's husband?" Liam asked, as he struggled to get comfortable in the seat.

"Didn't have time. I sent a message to Richard asking for whatever he can find." The Airbus A320 had in-flight Wi-Fi, so Aidan did some more digging as they sped through the center of the country. He couldn't find much more than additional information on Darius Ashoori's business.

Edwin had mentioned something about Darius doing some "shady" business in New York. Aidan pulled up an article on the influence of the Gambino family on the city's fashion industry. They used strong-arm tactics to control transporting goods from Seventh Avenue manufacturers to the sewing shops in which the garments were produced. It was likely that Darius had some connection to the mob back then, but eventually most of the goods began to be produced off-shore, eliminating that need for local truckers. And by 2024, most of those old mobsters were dead or imprisoned.

Unless they were sunning themselves in Boca Raton in their old age. Could one of them be carrying a grudge against Darius? Was he talking to one of them on his covert phone calls, worrying about an old contact coming after him?

The "fasten seat belts" sign came back on and Aidan abandoned his search. But once they arrived at the Charles de Gaulle airport in Paris, he was able to check his messages and find that Richard had put together a basic dossier and emailed it to both of them.

They sat in the Air France departure lounge and read. "Darius Ashoori was born in 1958 in Teheran, Iran. He studied fashion design at the University of Teheran and graduated in 1979. He moved to Paris, where he interned at the fashion house of Balmain. After four years there, he moved to New York, where he worked for Diane von Furstenberg for five years before starting his own clothing line, focused on high-end women's dresses."

Aidan looked up as a fashionable young woman in high heels with cork soles passed by. She was skinny as a runway model, and her floral print dress was tight to her body. Was she wearing an Ashoori, he wondered? Or would today's fashionistas even remember his name?

He went back to Richard's report. "Ashoori quickly became a society favorite and his dresses were regularly featured in high-fashion magazines and were worn by style-conscious women such as Diana Vreeland, Jacqueline Kennedy Onassis, and Gloria Vanderbilt. He sold his eponymous firm to a conglomerate in 2012 and retired to Boca Raton with his husband, Edwin Gallagher."

Aidan looked at Liam, who finished reading at the same time. "Well, that's a pretty bare bones summary," Aidan said. "I expect we will get the full run-down when he has time. I asked for whatever he can find on finances, criminal record, and health."

A pair of women in head-to-toe burkas passed by, accompanied by four small children and a burly guard in a black suit. One of the boys carried a small backpack with the Emirati flag on it, bars of green, white, and black, with a red column to the left. A month before, he and Liam could have been that guard, assigned to look after a family of wealthy tourists. Today they were on their way to flip the narrative, protecting a man in his own home.

"I'm concerned," Liam said. "On the surface Ashoori is a wealthy retiree. The police might be correct in assuming that this is a crime of opportunity—follow a rich guy and steal from him. But the way he was killed says something very different."

"Could it be that the killers meant to rob him after shooting him, but were scared away by those two witnesses?"

"It's not the way I expect a robbery to go down," Liam said. "You have to recognize that, too. We've studied the ways that people need to be protected. If you want to rob a rich guy, you wait until he's isolated, then you demand he hand over his wallet, his jewelry, all those shopping bags."

"That's why we tell clients not to flaunt their purchases," Aidan said. "Ask for plain bags instead of ones with the store logo. Be careful of their surroundings."

"If we approach this as if Ashoori was targeted for murder, we've got a very different story. The question becomes who wanted him dead?"

"Balzac said that behind every great fortune lies a great crime," Aidan said. "Maybe it was someone in his business." He told Liam what he'd read online about Mafia threats to the garment industry.

"But Ashoori retired ten years ago," Liam said. "And it doesn't look like he has been hiding."

"People hold grudges for a long time," Aidan said. "And it's possible that Darius did something to put a Mafioso in prison, and the guy was only recently released."

Liam nodded. "Good point. Our focus has to be protecting the client. If we figure out why Ashoori was murdered, then we know what cousin Eddie is up against."

"Edwin," Aidan said, and then the gate agent called for boarding their flight to Miami.

Aidan had booked them into business class on the transatlantic flight because that was part of the standard contract between the Agence de Securité and their clients. Usually they didn't travel farther than from one end of the Côte d'Azur to the other, so it was something special to be able to stretch out and relax in the more comfortable seats.

It was also a necessity for Liam, whose six-four frame did not fit into coach seats. He could do it, of course, but as he neared fifty the aches and pains of being crunched for ten hours would affect his ability to perform. When a client's life was at stake, it was better to spend a few extra bucks.

They were served lunch, and then everything was cleared away and the cabin's lights were dimmed. "Stop fidgeting and go to sleep," Liam grumbled.

"I'm trying."

"Feel heat at the top of your head," Liam said, as if he was reciting from a book. "Then let that warmth flow down through your body, bit by bit. As you do, relax. I can tell you're holding your hands stiffly."

Aidan leaned his seat back a few degrees and nestled down into it, trying to follow Liam's instructions. His husband's voice was quiet and soothing, like listening to a meditation tape. He didn't even realize when he'd fallen asleep, and only woke when they turned the cabin lights up for landing.

"Wow," he said, as he stretched. "I slept well."

"Thank the Navy," Liam said. "Have you been to Florida before?"

"Senior class trip to Disney World, a hundred years ago," Aidan said. "All I remember is long lines, bad food, and excessive heat."

"That describes the general Florida experience," Liam said. "Though I've only been to Navy bases in Jacksonville and Key West." He held up his hand. "And before you ask, I was still deep in the closet when my team went to Key West for deep-sea training. I wouldn't have been caught dead in a gay bar back then."

"Sometimes I think I was lucky that I fell in love with Blake when I was so young," Aidan said. "I avoided the grind of looking for sex in gay bars, and because Blake and I were monogamous we minimized the risk of getting AIDS."

"I don't have much good to say about Blake Chennault,"

Liam said. "He was a dick and he didn't treat you the way you deserve."

"That's sweet," Aidan said. "I didn't know any better until I met you."

The plane descended through the clouds and began to shake. The pilot made a sharp turn that sent Aidan's shoulder into Liam's and he grabbed the armrest. A rocky landing was only the first step in discovering why Edwin McCullough's husband had been killed, and what they could do to protect him.

Chapter 4

Anti-Aging

Liam

The Miami airport was crowded with Latin Americans returning home with heaped suitcases full of clothing for resale and Midwesterners on their way to Caribbean cruises. Aidan and Liam navigated their way to baggage claim and retrieved their luggage, then followed the signs to Customs. "Edwin said that at least we'll miss rush hour," Aidan said as they joined the end of a long line.

"Rush hour in Miami goes from three o'clock to seven-thirty or eight," the man ahead of them said. "Where are you headed?"

"Boca Raton," Aidan said.

"Rat's Mouth," the man said. "That's what it means in Spanish. But you'll never hear anyone who lives there call it that."

"It does sound prettier in Spanish," Aidan said. "I take it you don't live there?"

The man shook his head. "Delray Beach. Boca's poorer cousin. You guys on vacation?"

"Visiting family," Liam said.

Edwin had told them he was rattling around in a four-bedroom house, so he had plenty of room to put them up. And that he'd feel safer if they were in the house with him.

Liam agreed that was best. He and Aidan would have to scope out the property first, but usually a single-family house in a gated community was a safe place to lie low with a client.

They shuffled forward, showed their passports and their declaration statements, then found the rental car counter. Once again, the Agence contract specified an SUV because it rode high, gave good visibility and was generally safer than a sedan. Plus it suited Liam's long legs.

"I'll let you drive," Liam said when they reached the SUV. "I'll navigate."

The man in the Customs line was right; traffic on I-95 was heavy out of the city, though it eased somewhat after they passed through Fort Lauderdale. Boca Largo, the gated community where Edwin lived, was inside the city boundaries of Boca Raton. It was several miles west of the Turnpike along Glades Road, and night had fallen by the time they approached the turn for it.

"Wall around the exterior," Liam said. "That's good, but you and I will have to survey the exterior of the property and identify any weaknesses."

They pulled up beside the gatehouse. Liam was pleased to see both an arm and a gate preventing entry until the guard allowed. To the right was the residents' entry, controlled by a security system.

Aidan handed his French driver's license to the uniformed Black woman. "Oh, *vous êtes Français!*" she said, in what Liam recognized as a Haitian accent.

"No, American," Aidan said. "We live in France, though."

She turned to her computer and a moment later they heard Edwin Gallagher's recorded voice. "I'm expecting William McCullough and Aidan Greene. Please give them a pass for a week."

The guard handed Aidan a piece of green paper with his driver's license photo and the expiry date, along with his license. "*Profitez de votre séjour,*" she said.

"*Merci,*" he said, and once the gate opened he followed the directions printed on the screen past house after house that looked similar, all in a Mediterranean style, with terra-cotta tile roofs, arched doorways, and decorative ironwork. Much fancier than anything they'd see back in the south of France.

The area was well-landscaped, with lots of towering palm trees and flowering beds. Good sightlines, though, so there were few places for someone to hide behind bushes.

Aidan turned onto Gentle Rain Drive, moving slowly as they assessed house numbers. Each home was on a large lot with a broad driveway and the same lush landscaping.

They pulled up in the driveway of Edwin's house. It was a two-story villa with a two-car garage and well-lit windows. The front door opened and a man stood framed in the light. "Dumb and dumber," Liam said, as he jumped out of the SUV. He hurried up to the front door. "Edwin, get inside," he said. "You're making yourself into a target. Keep the door closed until we bring our bags up."

"Nice to see you, too," Edwin muttered, but he followed Liam's directions.

Liam returned to the SUV and Aidan began handing him luggage. "I hope you were polite," Aidan said.

"I told him the truth. Sometimes you have to shake people up to get them to listen." He didn't mention that he hadn't been as polite to his long-lost cousin as he could have been.

"Well, that's a start," Aidan said.

They walked up to the doorstep, tugging their rollaboard bags, and Edwin stood back to let them in. Liam was sure that his mother would have a few choice words for the décor inside the home Edwin had shared with Darius. Bordello would have been among the first. The word fairy would have popped in there, too, and not about Tinkerbell.

The floor was polished marble, and every wall was covered with framed photos. Looking more closely, Liam realized they were not family, or probably even friends. They all appeared to be photos of women wearing fancy dresses, probably designed by Darius Ashoori.

"I know, it's a shrine," Edwin said. "Darius was very proud of all that he accomplished."

"They're beautiful," Aidan said, and Liam wasn't sure if he meant the outfits or the women modeling them. To him, the women looked anorexic and the clothes bordered on the outlandish—but he'd seen a lot of both in France.

"It's so good to see you again, Bill--I mean Liam," Edwin said. "I don't get the chance to see cousins as much as I would like. Did you know Julia has six kids. Six!"

"I don't know who that is," Liam said.

"She's Aunt Diane's daughter. Your mother's older sister?"

"I think I know who Aunt Diane is," Liam said. "She was way older than my mother, wasn't she? I can't even remember if I ever met her."

"Our grandparents were teenagers when she was born," Edwin said. "If you look at the family tree you see her birthdate is only six months after the wedding. You can imagine the scandal!"

Liam couldn't, because his grandparents were blurry figures from his childhood. He didn't know any of the others, not Aunt Diane or any of her six grandchildren. He was almost insulted that Edwin assumed he knew or cared about these people, who were so far back in his past they could have been tintypes on a wall.

"We're here for a job, Edwin. Take us through the house so we can make sure it's secure."

Edwin looked like Hayam after she'd been chastised for digging in the back yard, but he said, "Certainly."

"Do you have an alarm system?"

"Do we live in Boca?" Edwin asked. "Of course. Let me show you how to arm and disarm it." He moved to a panel by the front door and keyed in the codes, which Liam memorized.

"Aidan, you wait here," Liam said. "I'm going to open every window and door and I want you to make sure they're all connected to this panel."

He and Edwin walked through all the downstairs rooms, and Liam opened each window and door in turn. Aidan called out the zone numbers as he did. Then he repeated the process with each room there. He noted the new glass in the back door approvingly.

"You're very thorough," Edwin said as they walked upstairs. "You get that from the McCullough side. My father was a real stickler for details and I inherited it, too."

"Uh-huh," Liam said, worried that next Edwin would start talking about the genetic basis of homosexuality and asking if he was a top or a bottom. He smirked to himself about the way Doris would have reacted to questions like that.

"Darius snored like a freight train," Edwin said as they

walked into the master bedroom. "So I sleep in the master suite built downstairs. You can use his room."

The bed was a massive four-poster, hung with short drapes on the sides. At least a dozen embroidered silk pillows were mounded at the head. All the furniture looked like it could have come from Versailles. Every piece was decorated within an inch of its life, with swags and curlicues and inlaid wood of different colors. There was more gold trim than Liam had seen in one place outside a museum.

He couldn't imagine sleeping there. Maybe he could stay in the small third bedroom on the second floor, though it only had a single bed, and he'd miss having Aidan beside him.

Once Liam was satisfied that every alarm sensor on the upper level worked, they went back downstairs, where he and Aidan retrieved their backpacks and suitcases, then climbed back up again.

"I'll give you fresh sheets and towels," Edwin said. "I haven't had the heart to clear out Darius's belongings. Maybe you can help me with that."

"I can," Aidan said. "I know it's a difficult thing to do."

"He'd want me to donate his clothes to a thrift store," Edwin said as he continued walking. "Spread the designer love around."

Liam was glad that Aidan was there to act as a buffer for Edwin's deep sadness. He'd never been that great with emotion. Living with a father who was a drunk had trained him to bury those feelings, and it was only with Aidan that he had learned to express some of them.

In addition to being naturally empathetic, Aidan had spent years teaching immigrants the rudiments of English. He'd lived with them through their traumas, their uncertainty about their new lives, and all the pain of adjustment. He was much better at emotion than Liam would ever be.

Aidan got to Darius's bedroom first, and Liam heard him gasp. He knew why.

"It's certainly breathtaking," Aidan said.

"Very Darius," Edwin said. "When I slept here with him I was afraid I'd wake up to find Marie Antoinette beside me."

"Not Louis the Sixteenth?"

Edwin laughed. "Oh, honey, you have no idea." He seemed to look at them for the first time. "You're both very butch, aren't you? I may not look very masculine but I was the man in our relationship, if you know what I mean. Darius liked to wear silk and lace undies."

"That's a little too much information too soon," Liam said.

"Oh, yes," Edwin said. "I'm sorry. I'm still trying to wrap my head around what happened." He walked over to the bed. "But you know what, I hated most of this frippery. Liam, you're tall. Can you take down the swags alongside the bed? I'll be right back."

When he was gone, Liam turned to Aidan and in a low voice said, "You wanted to come here. I'm trying but I cannot see any way that man is my relation."

"That's because you're treating him like a client, instead of a cousin. And he needs our help. Now reach up and take down those swags."

Liam obeyed. By the time he was done, Edwin had returned with a stack of sheets and towels and a giant black trash bag. "Hold this," he said to Liam.

He turned to the bed and began tossing the decorative pillows into the bag. "I hated these. I used to think I would lose my mind if he brought another ruffle into the house."

When the bag was full, he and Aidan began stripping the bed. Liam looked into the bathroom then asked, "Okay if I clear out some of the toiletries? We'll need some room to put out our own stuff."

"Feel free. There's already a trash can in there."

The bathroom smelled of lavender and something spicy Liam couldn't identify. The floor was marble and the fixtures looked like Martha Stewart had swept through. The wallpaper was a repeating pattern of geishas doing their makeup.

At least the shower enclosure was a glass one. In their guest bathroom, Slava and Thierry had a tub with a curtain of a trio of Tom of Finland men enjoying the shower spray together.

That probably wouldn't have fit with Darius's sense of style, though.

The medicine cabinet was full of prescription bottles. He set them aside to drop off at a local pharmacy because he knew it wasn't healthy to toss it all in the trash. Then he turned to all the toiletries. Body oil, pore cleanser, a special cleaner for pubic hair. Charcoal face wash, eye stick, lip balm, face mask, Chinese pads to remove the toxins from the bottoms of your feet.

The anti-aging moisturizer made him sad. Darius hadn't lived to enjoy the benefits.

Chapter 5

Dark Places

Liam

By the time he returned to the bedroom, with a wastebasket full of half-used beauty products, Aidan and Edwin had changed the sheets. The bedspread that looked like a Fragonard painting was gone, replaced by a simple one patterned with sailboats.

Edwin had cleared the top of the bureau, too. "Let's move Darius's clothes to the spare bedroom," Edwin said, and they began carrying armloads of shirts, slacks, and suits from the closet to a smaller bedroom down the hall.

"You're going to have to deliver something to the funeral home once you have the service set up," Aidan said. "Did Darius have a favorite suit? Something it would be nice to bury him in?"

Edwin stopped at the entrance to the bedroom. "He designed a suit to wear the day he sold the business," he said. "Typical Darius. He had to control everything. He had his favorite tailor prepare it and he did the finishing touches himself. The embroidery along the collar and the cuffs. And he stitched his initials into the lining of the jacket."

"Where's that suit now?"

"At the end of the rack," Edwin said. "Can we leave that here? Would you mind?"

"Not at all."

They finished carrying everything else out, though Aidan made sure to leave the right accessories to go with the suit—a white shirt with matching embroidery, down to silk socks and boxers.

"I'm glad we did that," Edwin said when the closet was empty. "Cathartic. Next step is to get it all in the car and out of the house."

He smiled weakly. "Well, I'll leave you boys to get settled. Esmeralda will be here tomorrow at nine, just so you know."

"Esmeralda?" Liam asked. He wouldn't be surprised if Edwin and Darius employed a woman to come in dressed like the gypsy girl in *The Hunchback of Notre Dame*.

"We call her the cleaning lady, but as you've seen the house is so full of stuff it's hard for her to get to any surface. At least she cleans the toilets."

With that, he left.

"Your mother would have a heart attack the minute she walked into this house," Aidan said. "I wonder how close Edwin is to Aunt Doris."

"Probably as close as I am," Liam said. "It looks like we'll be here for a while, so we might as well unpack."

They worked together, Aidan hanging up the clothes and Liam laying out their toiletries and their electronics. Then Aidan yawned.

"I'm beat," he said. "I'm going to take a shower and then go to sleep."

"I'll take a quick run," Liam said. "Get the lay of the land."

"Be careful. It's ten o'clock at night."

"Yes, mother."

Liam quickly changed into his running clothes and stopped at the open door of Edwin's first-floor bedroom. His cousin sat on the edge of the bed staring at his iPad.

"I'm going out for a quick run. You have a house key I can use?"

Edwin looked up. "This late?"

Liam repressed a sigh. "I'd like to see what the place looks like at night."

"They roll up the sidewalks at eight," Edwin said. "Half the people in this community can't see to drive after dark. But be my guest."

He led Liam back to the front door and picked a key out of a drawer. The chain had a charm in what looked like the shape of a country. He looked at it.

"Iran," Edward said. "Or Persia, as Darius preferred to call it. Along with many other things, he was obsessed with his homeland and the idea that one day the people would rise up and topple the theocracy and he could go home again."

Edwin smiled again, that same smile that didn't reach the edges of his mouth. "But as Thomas Wolfe said, you can't go home again. Especially not if your home puts gay people to death."

And on that cheery note, Liam thought, as he slipped the keychain in his pocket.

Liam took a good look at his cousin then as they walked to the front door. He had the same oval face that Doris did, the same mousy brown hair. Liam had always been told he looked like his father, Big Bill, but that he had Doris's smile. He looked at Edwin's face but couldn't see a resemblance to his own.

Liam punched the code in to set the alarm, then took off

down the sidewalk to the street. The air was cool and humid, and the only sounds were the rumble of air conditioning compressors and the distant noise of a truck bouncing over a speed bump. It was too dark to check for any gaps in the wall around the community, but Liam thought the best way to get the sense of a place was on foot.

A few stars poked through the light cloud cover. An occasional car passed him on Boca Largo Promenade, the main street that connected all the cul-de-sacs. Streetlights were infrequent and irregular, and there were many dark places where someone could hide unseen by passing cars or security guards.

In his experience, people in communities like Boca Largo had a weakened sense of what kept them secure. They thought a wall, a gate and a guard protected them. Many of the people in the community probably never armed their alarm systems. Darius Ashoori had thought so little of his personal security that he was willing to drive a Rolls Royce and flaunt his wealth.

And look where it had gotten him.

Liam ran for about half an hour, and never saw a security guard in a roving car. A man giving his golden retriever a last walk before bedtime, a solitary car moving slowly down the street with its high beams on, the driver barely visible behind the steering wheel. Almost every house was dark, though most had some kind of light outside, either over a garage or uplighting a collection of palms.

When he returned to the house on Gentle Rain Drive, he disarmed the alarm and then set it again. Edwin's door was closed and the light out.

He climbed the stairs to the second floor. Aidan was sitting up in bed reading. "What did you think of the community?"

"Let me take a quick shower."

The bathroom still smelled like a mix of Darius's cosmetics, so Liam hurried in and out. "Do you know, he had six different razors?" he asked. "Four electric, two straight. Probably the only straight things in this house."

"Including us," Aidan said.

Liam joined Aidan in bed naked, sliding under the covers. "We're probably safe enough in this community." He told Aidan what he'd seen. "I'll do a better recon in the morning."

He turned on his side and went quickly to sleep. When he woke on Wednesday morning the sun was beginning to rise over the rooftops across the street, and he put on a jock strap, a fresh pair of shorts, and a tank top, and let himself quietly out of the house.

Edwin had given him a map of the community, and his first project was to make sure there were no gaps in the wall that would let an assassin in.

He felt silly using that word—but then, Darius's death had been an assassination. If his killer was after Edwin as well, it paid to be safe. He jogged slowly down Gentle Rain Drive to where it connected to Boca Largo Promenade. The area must have been swampland at the edge of the Everglades once upon a time, because it was dotted with small lakes and cul-de-sacs that gave almost every home a water view.

Many Boca Largo residents got an early start. Liam passed men on three-wheeled bicycles, power-walking women and even a few joggers as he continued along the Promenade. Boca Largo was a fifty-five and older community, but plastic surgery and modern medicine kept the people he passed looking younger.

He tried to parallel the wall, but in many cases it ran

behind someone's house so the best he could do was take a quick look as he ran up and down the cul-de-sacs, but he didn't draw any attention.

The counter to that was that anyone trying to harm Edwin probably wouldn't draw notice either.

Chapter 6

Police Visit
Aidan

Aidan was in the kitchen when Liam returned from his morning run. "Edwin isn't much of a cook," he said. "We'll have to do a grocery run. But I found ingredients to make pancakes."

"Chocolate chips?"

Aidan shook his head. "For some reason there was a package of cinnamon chips in the cupboard. They'll have to do."

By the time Liam had showered and changed into a polo shirt and a pair of 511 tactical shorts, which had enough pockets to stow any necessary gear, Edwin was in the kitchen with Aidan, and there were pancakes on the griddle. "This is a real treat," Edwin said. "Either we had protein shakes for breakfast or we went out to a local deli."

"For now you're safest staying in the house," Liam said as he sat down across from his cousin. "Is that going to be a problem for you?"

Edwin shook his head. "I was always Mr. Inside while Darius was Mr. Outside. I'm happiest by myself reading a book."

He and Liam didn't fit that pattern, Aidan thought, as he flipped the pancakes. Liam liked to get out and run, though he preferred to be solitary when he did so. Aidan was happiest when settled down with a book, though he preferred to have Liam and Hayam in the same room. Aidan was better with clients, empathizing with them, while Liam tended to be didactic in his instructions.

But they both had friends, and liked to travel, stay in hotels, and eat in restaurants. Ever since their first adventure through the Sahara, they had found that their differences complemented each other, while their similarities drew them together.

Aidan served everyone pancakes with butter and what looked like an ancient bottle of maple syrup. "How did you and Darius meet?" he asked, as he sat down.

"When I graduated from Hofstra, I wanted a job with a touch of glamour," Edwin said, as he forked a piece of pancake. "So I headed to the rag district in New York. I went to every showroom and manufacturer and left a resume, and I lucked out that I was there when one of the clerks was fired. I got the job and worked my way up to office manager."

He ate for a moment. "These are delicious," he said to Aidan. "Oh, you wanted to know how I met Darius. I spent my twenties looking for Mr. Right Now. My job was boring but I learned a lot about the business of fashion—the different kinds of fabrics, offshore manufacturing, all that kind of stuff. Occasionally I'd snag an invitation to one of the big parties, but I was such a mouse no one paid attention to me."

He smiled, and Aidan noticed that it covered his whole face. "Until I went to a party for a big brand, and found myself next to Darius in the line for the bar. I didn't know who he was then—he was one of the designers at Diane von Furstenberg. I said something snarky about one of the designs on display, and Darius laughed."

Aidan listened intently. He loved this kind of story, and relished telling people how he and Liam had met, emphasizing that Liam was naked the first time Aidan saw him.

"He said something back to me, and we started to chat, and it was as if the world fell away and it was just the two of us. I went home with him that night and the sex was glorious, and within a few months I was living with him. I was so certain that he was talented that I encouraged him to start his own label. I went with him to meet every investor, and Darius charmed them and showed his designs, and I backed him up with all the business information."

He shrugged. "That was that, until he decided he wanted to retire. He sold the business within a few months and we moved down here."

"What did you think of that?" Aidan asked.

"I wasn't ready to retire. I was the controller of a fashion house in Manhattan. We had a very active social life—the Met Gala, Fashion Week, and everything else. But Darius had this idea he wanted to start over again."

"Do you think that could be connected to his death?" Liam asked. "Aidan and I did some research on Ashoori Industries and we turned up rumors of mob connections."

Edwin waved his hand. "The mob controlled the trucking industry back then. If you wanted your materials to come in on time, and your clothes to ship without problems, you had to deal with them. It was a business expense, like paying customs duties on imported fabric. No one ever threatened us."

"Did Darius ever testify at a trial?" Aidan asked. "We

thought maybe a mobster was recently released from prison and ended up down here, with a grudge against Darius."

"Neither of us were ever involved in a trial," Edwin said. "But we did know some of those men socially. A couple of the capos would show up at industry parties, parading around younger girlfriends with augmented breasts."

He placed his silverware on his plate. "Darius told me that he once sucked one of them off in a men's room, but it's not like he would have been forced. And he never mentioned anyone from that world after we left New York."

What a world, Aidan thought. He'd once met a client of Blake's who was later arrested for bribery, who had an Italian last name and a reputed connection to the Bruno crime family. The man had seemed supremely ordinary, and Blake had been as surprised as he was.

Edwin stood and carried his empty plate to the sink. "And here we were, for ten years."

"What did you do with yourselves?" Liam asked.

"We had a very active social life," Edwin said. "Concerts, art galleries, theater. Darius was very gregarious, as I've said. He made friends everywhere. I've been besieged with condolence emails and texts, though no one has come over to the house or asked how I'm doing. Maybe it's because I haven't been able to have a funeral yet. The police are still holding onto Darius's body."

He sighed. "I'm coming to realize most of the people we knew were attracted by Darius's personality, and I was an accessory."

Aidan began to clean up. He believed their friends were attracted to both of them, but what would happen if Liam died? Would he be on his own? He couldn't imagine Slava and Thierry leaving him alone. They'd be at the house every minute. Thierry would cook and bake himself into a frenzy.

The doorbell rang. "Expecting anyone?" Liam asked.

Edwin shook his head. "And I haven't been called by the front gate to authorize any visitors. Must be a neighbor."

"I'll check it out," Liam said.

Aidan followed him to the front window, where the shades were closed. Liam tweaked them open a bit and then said, "There's a black sedan outside. Looks like it might be an unmarked police car."

"The police don't have to get approval to come in," Edwin said. "I've learned that."

Liam went to the door and opened it a crack. From behind him Aidan saw a middle-aged Asian woman in a navy business suit carrying several shopping bags. She juggled the bags to retriever her wallet. She opened it and showed an ID to Liam. "I'm here to see Mr. Gallagher," she said.

Liam stepped back. "Come in."

"You are?" she asked, before she stepped inside.

"Liam McCullough. I'm Mr. Gallagher's cousin. That's my husband, Aidan Greene."

She stuck out her hand. "Pleased to meet you. I'm Detective Tseng from the Boca Raton Police. I'm investigating Mr. Ashoori's death."

She shook hands with Aidan and then turned to Edwin. "Once again, Mr. Gallagher, my profound condolences on your loss. I wanted to stop by personally and bring you up to date on my investigation."

"Thank you."

She tried to hand him the shopping bags, but Edwin stepped back. Aidan took them instead. "Why don't I leave these in the garage," he said.

Edwin nodded. Aidan dashed to the garage and returned to find them in the living room, which was as overdecorated as every other room in the house. Plump sofas slip-covered in fabric patterned with tropical birds. A rococo coffee table and matching end tables. Large cloisonne vases filled with artificial flowers.

"Do you want your cousins here?" Detective Tseng asked.

"Yes, please. They're also serving as my bodyguards, so it's important that they know everything."

She raised an eyebrow. "Bodyguards?"

"I believe that Darius was deliberately murdered, and until I know why I asked Liam and Aidan to come stay with me."

"I understand how you feel," Tseng said. "But we have no reason to believe anything other than that your husband was the victim of a failed smash-and-grab."

"Why didn't the killer take anything, then?" Liam asked.

Tseng shrugged. "Many crimes of opportunity like this one are committed on the spur of the moment, without a lot of thought or planning. It's possible that the perpetrator didn't intend to kill Mr. Ashoori at all, but something spooked him. Then he was too frightened to carry out the theft."

"My understanding is that Mr. Ashoori was killed by two bullets to the head," Liam said. "Aidan and I have been in personal protection for quite a while, and we both have had extensive training. That kind of shooting implies deliberate murder, doesn't it?"

"It may. Or as I said, it could be someone nervous and inexperienced."

They talked for a few more minutes, but it was clear

that Detective Tseng's mind was made up. "We're interviewing people we have arrested for similar crimes in the past. We have feelers out to a variety of sources. We'll let you know when we make any progress."

"What about the car the killer drove?" Aidan asked. "Any luck there?"

Tseng shook her head. "The witnesses were in a different lane of the parking lot and couldn't see a license plate or even give us a definitive make and model."

"Just curious," Liam asked. "Any reports of stolen cars in the time shortly before Mr. Ashoori's shooting?"

"I'd have to get back to you on that," Tseng said. She pulled out her phone and made a note.

"And of course if one of those stolen cars was abandoned soon after," Liam added.

"I see where you're going. But even if we find a stolen vehicle that matches the timetable, there's still no way to connect it to Mr. Ashoori's death."

"When will I be able to have Darius's funeral?" Edwin asked. "He was Jewish, though he wasn't very observant, but Jews like to do their burials quickly."

She stood up. "I'll check with the coroner's office. Thank you for your time. I'll be in touch."

Edwin rose and showed her out.

"What do you think?" Aidan asked, while Edwin was out of the room.

"She's got a narrow focus, though I believe she'll do what's necessary. But I don't believe that her methods are going to turn up Darius's killer, or relieve Edwin's fears."

Chapter 7

Six Million

Liam

"She seems very nice," Edwin said, when he came back to the living room. "I hope she's right, and that Darius's death was a horrible accident. But I don't believe it."

"We have our suspicions, too," Liam said.

Aidan rose. "Is there a grocery nearby? I'd like to bring in some provisions."

"There's a Whole Foods on Glades Road, on the other side of 95," Edwin said. "That's where we shopped when we needed anything. I'll give you a credit card."

The cleaning lady, a petite Latina in jeans and a T-shirt, arrived, and she headed upstairs to do what she could.

While Aidan worked up a grocery list with Edwin, Liam checked their laptop for any messages. There was one from Richard, but it was very brief.

"Suspicious pattern of payments from one of Ashoori's accounts at Fidelity," Richard wrote. "Might want to ask the husband about those. Money went to an offshore account in the Cayman Islands, so will be harder to trace."

Great, Liam thought.

"Also found an email account in his name with Proton Mail. That's going to be tough to hack, so see if the husband has the password for that. More to come."

That was all.

By the time he finished reading, Aidan was on his way out with the shopping list. "I've got a couple of questions for you, Edwin," Liam said. "Did Darius have an office here in the house?"

"He did. I'll take you up there."

Esmeralda had already finished with the office and Liam heard her singing a Spanish song as she worked in the master suite.

The office was surprisingly spare considering the rest of the house. A large mahogany desk, several wood-paneled filing cabinets, and a couple of comfortable chairs. The walls were lined with photographs, many of them of Darius with a very aristocratic-looking woman.

"One of his customers?" he asked Edwin.

"The Shahbanu," he said. "Widow of the late Shah of Iran. Farah Pahlavi to ordinary people like you and me." He joined Liam at the wall. "Those were all dresses Darius designed. He and the Shahbanu were very close. Whenever she came to New York she'd go to his salon and they'd gossip in Farsi. She said he was one of her closest friends."

"Really? Have you heard from her?"

Edwin shook his head. "I suppose I should get a message to her. I'm sure she'll be devastated."

"We have a computer expert who's been looking into Darius's affairs to see if we can identify a reason why someone might want to have him killed," Liam said. "He discovered that Darius has been making some large payments to an offshore account from his Fidelity account. Do you know anything about that?"

Edwin shook his head. "We don't have an account with Fidelity."

"Richard usually gets this stuff right. Do you have the password for Darius's computer?"

"I do. 090179. The date Darius left Iran for Paris."

"Do you mind?" Liam asked, motioning to the desk.

"Go ahead."

Liam sat down and turned on the computer, an expensive Microsoft Surface laptop. The machine didn't recognize his face, so it prompted him for his login. He typed the date in and the splash screen came up. "Our researcher came up with a Proton Mail email account in Darius's name," Liam said. "Is that the company you both used?"

Edwin shook his head. "We both used Gmail for everything."

Liam searched Darius's desktop screen for a link to Proton Mail. It was so cluttered with notes and files and links that he had trouble scanning through everything. "Ah, there it is," he said. It was a small icon almost hidden by another bigger one. He clicked on it, and when the software came up, he tried the password Edwin had given him. It didn't work.

"Any other passwords Darius might have used?"

"He wasn't the most tech-savvy guy," Edwin said. "I tried to get him to use different passwords but he refused."

Liam hit a couple of keys to view saved passwords on the computer, but there wasn't one listed for Proton Mail. Probably the system had been instructed not to save it.

There were three options to recover a lost password. Liam entered the Gmail address Darius used and then crossed his fingers, but all he got was a screen that said if the email was registered, a message would be sent to reset the password.

He turned to Edwin. "Do you have Darius's phone? We could get a code for Proton Mail through it."

"I don't."

"While we're waiting for that email to come through, let's look at Fidelity," Liam said. A user ID was displayed there, but Liam needed a password. Since Edwin didn't even know the account existed, he wouldn't know what that was. So Liam went back to the saved passwords, and found one for Fidelity. He hit the drop-down arrow to reveal the password.

It was S3cr3t. "Not a very secret password, is it?" he said, more to himself than to his cousin.

"That's magic," Edwin said from over his shoulder.

"Not really." Liam logged in and saw that Edwin had an account with Fidelity with a balance of over six million dollars.

"You didn't know about this?" Liam asked.

"I didn't. And I handled all the money. Darius was 'creative,' he always said, so he didn't have much concept of money."

Liam didn't believe his cousin. "Six million dollars is a lot for you not to know about."

Edwin frowned. "Darius sold his company for a mix of cash and shares of the stock in Strada Fashion Holdings, the company that bought him out. The total was something north of twelve million. We took in about six in cash, which went into our joint accounts. The rest was in Strada stock. As far as I know, we still hold that stock. I'll have to get to my computer to check it out."

Liam pointed to the screen. "There's the pattern of transfers Darius was making. You have no idea what he was doing?"

"Not at all."

"Could it be blackmail?"

"For what?" Edwin asked. "We were a pair of old queens in our sunset years. Why would anyone blackmail us?"

"I hate to pry." Liam especially hated to ask about sexual details, and usually managed to leave that up to Aidan. But his husband was out shopping. "How was your sex life?"

"Like any old couple, I guess," Edwin said. "We didn't usually do more than the occasional cuddle or kiss on New Year's Eve."

"Could Darius have found someone else?"

Edwin moved around the desk and sat down hard on the facing chair. Liam watched his eyes twitch back and forth as he thought about the possibility that his dead husband was cheating on him.

He couldn't imagine how he'd feel if he was in his cousin's shoes. Aidan Greene was the best thing that had ever happened to him, and being with him was like air. Something he needed, couldn't live without.

"I'm not naïve. I know there are gay bars in the area, though not here in Boca. I didn't keep tabs on Darius twenty-four hours a day, so it's possible he was out dipping his wick occasionally, though he was very discreet."

"Never arrested for anything?" Liam asked.

Edwin laughed. "Though Darius could be a sexual libertine, he was also very prudish and concerned about cleanliness. I can't see him doing anything more than giving a blow job in a back alley or a bathroom. I doubt he did anything worth being blackmailed for." He turned to Liam. "And if someone tried to extort money from me over something Darius did, I'd laugh, and he knew that."

He crossed his arms over his chest. "Although. Darius

started to be very cagey about six months ago. I had a sense that he was hiding something from me, but honestly, I thought it was something good. Like he'd been making plans for a surprise gift, maybe a cruise somewhere. I think I mentioned to you that occasionally he took phone calls outside, and sometimes he'd go out for the afternoon and wouldn't say where he was going."

"Did you ever confront him?"

Edwin shook his head. "I was waiting to see how things played out. Darius was very particular that way. He liked to do things his way and he got angry if I disrupted them."

Keeping secrets from your husband was never a good idea. Sure, Liam had told Aidan the occasional fib, to keep the peace. Yes, honey, that shirt looks good on you. Dinner was delicious.

But never anything as big as whatever secret Darius kept from Edwin. Had it been the cause of his death?

He opened Darius's Gmail account, and though he looked through a load of unopened messages in Primary, Promotions and Social, even in Spam, there was nothing from Proton Mail.

Whatever secrets Darius was hiding, he had done a good job of keeping them hidden.

Chapter 8

His Own Rules

Aidan

Aidan hadn't realized that his route to Whole Foods would take him past the Beer, Wine and More store where Darius was killed. A morbid curiosity drew him to swerve into the parking lot, causing the driver he cut in front of to blow his horn and swear.

He had no idea where the shooting had taken place, but the incident with the other driver made him wonder if Darius had been a victim of road rage. There were a lot of crazy drivers on the road, and one of them could have resented Darius's driving, or his ownership of a car that cost more than many peoples' homes.

He'd been guilty of such feelings himself in the past, refusing to let an expensive car merge in front of him in heavy traffic. But he'd never considered following the driver and shooting him.

He drove slowly through the parking lot, looking for bloodstains on the pavement, but couldn't spot any. The nighttime downpours had probably washed away any residue, but he still felt a chill, as if Darius's angry ghost was haunting the lot until his killers were caught.

After a few minutes he continued to Whole Foods, where he was astonished not only at the range of food available, but the prices. He was glad that he had Edwin's credit card in his pocket.

Not everyone had a neighbor with a greenhouse. He and Liam were very lucky. He stopped for a moment in the produce aisle, before a gorgeous display of peppers in a rainbow of colors, and realized he was even luckier. His husband was still alive.

That wasn't a revelation, but it still shook him.

"Excuse me? I need to get through."

He looked behind him. A woman Edwin would have called a Boca Babe with a cart loaded with bottles of vitamin supplements was right behind him, even though there was plenty of room for her to get around. "Sorry," he said, and pushed his cart forward, but not before he had a chance to survey her extensive plastic surgery.

He forced himself to focus on the food they needed, without worrying about the cost. The client was paying, and he had to cater three meals a day for three people.

By the time he finished, he had five large paper bags of groceries and a tab of over two hundred dollars. At the Boca Largo gate, he flashed the paper entry pass as he thought how easy it would be to forge one. It was a simple sheet of paper, faded as a result of multiple photocopying, with his name, Edwin's, and Edwin's address.

Another mark against the community's security.

He carried two bags up to the front door and once he was inside, he called, "Liam? Can you help with the groceries?"

Liam came down the stairs with his typical grace and soon all five bags were stacked on the granite countertop in the kitchen. "Buy enough food?" Liam asked.

"Don't get me started. Anything happen while I was away?"

"The cleaning lady was impressed with how we tidied up the master suite," Liam said. They began unpacking the bags and storing the food in the refrigerator and the cabinets.

"Do you think there's any chance that Darius was killed due to road rage?" he asked. He told Liam about his quick turn into the parking lot.

"While that's a possibility, I've been learning more about Mr. Ashoori," Liam said. "I looked at some of the investment websites with Edwin. Darius sold some stock he owned in the company that bought his operation, and used that to fund a secret account that started with something north of six million dollars. He's been making regular transfers of a hundred grand at a time to that Cayman bank Richard discovered."

"Blackmail?"

"That was my thought. I had to ask Edwin some uncomfortable questions."

"Let me guess. They haven't done the horizontal mambo in ages."

"Got it in one. And about six months ago, Darius started keeping secrets. Edwin didn't question him because Darius liked to do things his way, and surprise Edwin with cruises and gifts."

"How many transfers are we talking about?"

"One a month."

Aidan stopped on his way to the kitchen cabinet with a bag of flour in one hand and a canister of raisins in the other. "That's six hundred grand. A lot of money to pay to cover up some illicit nookie."

"I agree. But we don't know if it was blackmail at all."

Aidan continued putting away the food. "Other ideas?"

"Right now I'm stumped. We don't know enough about Darius to begin speculating."

"Could he have been buying antiques?" Aidan asked. "This house certainly has no shortage of knickknacks that look old as dirt."

"Smuggled goods, you mean?"

"Possibly. He was from Iran, after all. Maybe he had a connection there who was getting him some ancient artifacts."

"We'll have to quiz Edwin," Liam said.

"Quiz me about what?"

Aidan looked up to see Edwin the kitchen doorway. He wasn't sure what the client had heard—he hoped he'd missed the part about his and his husband's sex lives.

"You have a lot of what look like valuable antiques in your cabinets," Aidan said.

"Darius was a collector. Anything from Iran, and lots of Judaica, but pretty much anything that caught his eye."

"I'd love to see the Judaica," Aidan said. "Maybe after lunch?"

"Any time," Edwin said. Aidan had brought croissants, ham, and cheese, and made them sandwiches for lunch, accompanied by low-salt potato chips. As they were eating, Edwin's cell phone rang.

"It's the detective," he said. "Should I answer?"

"Of course," Liam said. "Can you put her on speaker so we can all hear?"

Edwin nodded, and after he said hello he asked if Liam and Aidan could listen in. When Detective Tseng agreed, Edwin hit a button. "You're on," he said.

"I wanted to let you know that the coroner's office is ready to release Mr. Ashoori's body."

"Thank you," Edwin said.

"And to follow up, I checked the security cameras at Boca Largo, and reports of stolen vehicles. Nothing from either source. I'll be in touch when I have anything else to tell you."

When they finished eating, Liam went back up to Darius's office and Edwin and Aidan walked out to the living room. "Would you mind sitting with me while I call the funeral home?"

"Not at all."

"He never said what he wanted, but I'll give him a Jewish funeral," Edwin said.

"I can help with that," Aidan said. "I'm Jewish, too."

"Oh, thank you. I found the name of a local funeral home and put it in my phone. Here it is."

Aidan thought Edwin was doing a good job of holding it together as they made the arrangements. Edwin had already decided to buy a double plot in a non-denominational cemetery. Aidan answered the questions Edwin couldn't, and they scheduled a service for Sunday afternoon. The home would take care of an announcement in the paper. "Will you be sitting shiva?" the clerk asked.

Aidan shook his head to Edwin, who said no.

The clerk ended the call with his condolences and Edwin hung up. "What did that mean? Sitting with Shiva?" Edwin asked. "I thought Shiva was an Indian god. Nothing to do with Jews."

"Shiva is a period of time when the family stays at home to receive mourners," Aidan said. "But for your safety, it's best to avoid that."

"Anyone who wanted to come over would have done so as soon as they heard about Darius," Edwin said. "And now, you wanted to see the collection."

He flicked a switch, and the glass cases that lined the room were illuminated. "Everything here is organized," Edwin said. "God forbid I happened to move something. Darius would have a fit."

He choked back a sob. "I'm still having trouble realizing he's never coming back."

Aidan put his arm around Edwin's shoulders. "I know it's a cliché, but it will get better."

Edwin nodded. "I know." He straightened up, and Aidan let him go. "Now this first cabinet is the Judaica. Darius had a half-dozen antique dealers on notice, and cartons would arrive without notice. Most of the time I didn't have any idea what he'd bought. Those silver boxes are spice containers. I particularly like the one with the little flag on top."

"They're for the Havdalah service on Saturday night," Aidan said. "The conclusion of the Sabbath."

"Oh, I always assumed they were for cooking," Edwin said. "Interesting."

He pointed out other items—enameled square boxes for tzedakah, or charity, and egg-shaped containers for the etrog, used at Sukkot. Aidan was surprised that Edwin knew so little about something that had mattered to his husband.

Aidan had spent years learning about the Navy SEALs —their teams, their patches, their specialties, because he knew that Liam was proud of his service. SEAL Team Four's slogan was "mad al osteo" – bad to the bone. SEAL Team Seven's was an inverted triangle with the number 7 in the middle. If he was ever on Jeopardy! and they had a category for Navy SEALs, he thought he'd be able to run it.

Eventually they moved on to other items. Aidan was particularly interested in the items that Edwin said represented the Persian empire. The stars of his collection were a gold bas-relief of a winged lion and a stone sculpture of a king with a crown and an elaborate dotted beard. There were other more prosaic items, like an inlaid stone mug and a small sculpture of a buxom reclining woman.

"It's like being in a museum," Aidan said.

Edwin nodded. "Darius wanted to donate his collection to a museum eventually but he hadn't gotten around to figuring out which one."

"Are any of these recent purchases?" Aidan asked.

"I'd have to look through his receipts. There is so much stuff here that he could have bought things and put them away without ever telling me." He nodded. "Liam said that Darius was sending a lot of money to a bank account in the Cayman Islands. Maybe it was for artifacts. It's illegal to bring things out of Iran now so he might have had to keep things secret."

"Was he generally a law-abiding guy?" Aidan asked.

Edwin laughed. "Darius had a unique approach to government, based on what happened to him and his family. We paid taxes on our income—I made sure of that. I didn't want either of us to end up in prison for tax evasion."

"But in other areas?"

"Well, let's say he had flexible ethics. Particularly when it came to Persia, or the Shahbanu, or anything related to his heritage. In those cases he made his own rules."

Edwin led him upstairs to Darius's office, where Liam had his reading glasses on and was leaning toward the computer screen. "The receipts for all the antiques are in the second file cabinet," Edwin said. "I'll leave you to it. I'd like to take a nap." He walked out.

"What are you looking at?" Aidan asked Liam.

"Darius's emails. The man never cleared out his junk. It's amazing."

"Find anything interesting?"

"Not yet. Did Edwin say anything about the antiques downstairs?"

"That Darius was a compulsive collector without much care about provenance. I'm going to look through the receipts and see if any of those hundred-grand payments went for tchotchkes."

"If Darius heard you call his antiques tchotchkes he'd probably have a fit."

"Good thing he's dead, then."

Aidan realized what he'd said. "Oops. Didn't mean that."

Chapter 9

Receipts

Liam

They spent most of Wednesday afternoon together in Darius's office. Liam steamrolled through the files in Darius's in-box, flagging only a few that looked worth following up. Aidan began a systematic review of all the invoices in the file cabinet, discovering to his dismay that Darius had done little to categorize them.

Most of them were in date order, at least, because it looked like Darius simply shoved them into the cabinet after he received the goods.

His filing represented his compulsive nature. He saved every copy of everything related to an object, even the torn envelope the invoice arrived in. Aidan sat on the floor of the office and began making piles of documents, trying to impose some sort of order. If Edwin wanted to sell anything, or donate it, he'd need to be able to find the appropriate paperwork.

"This is not what I expected to be doing when I started a business in close protection," Liam grumbled, halfway through the afternoon.

"Do you want to go for a run? I'll switch over to the emails and leave this paperwork for later."

Liam stared at the screen in frustration. "No, you keep doing what you're doing. How does anyone expect an email message to get through when there's so much spam? I can't tell you how many messages I've deleted about erectile dysfunction, limited time offers, and foreign nationals who have decided to donate their money to Darius."

"None of those foreign nationals happen to be Iranians, do they?" Aidan asked.

"That would be too easy. So far I've only flagged about a dozen messages that need following up. Almost all of them are from names that sound Iranian to me. Esfahani, Hashemi, Jahandar, and Pahlavi."

"The shah's last name was Pahlavi. Any messages from his widow or any of this children?"

"Nope. I did a quick search and discovered that it's a common last name, meaning older or earlier. But I'm keeping an eye on those. Probably send them to Richard for follow-up."

"We ought to ask him what he can find on the Shahbanu," Aidan said. "If he can find any connection between her and Darius beyond gossiping in Farsi during clothing fittings."

"Make a note," Liam said, and they went back to work.

Midway through the afternoon, a confirmation email came through from Proton Mail, allowing him to reset Darius's password to that secret account and get access to his emails.

"Fingers crossed this works, and leads us somewhere," Liam said, as Aidan joined him behind the computer. Liam created the new password, and Darius's inbox opened.

In an Arabic-style script Liam assumed was Persian.

Liam groaned. "This never gets easy, does it?"

"I can download an archive of the messages and then run them through a translation app," Aidan said. "I'd rather not copy them individually into Google translate. You never know who's listening to those."

Liam stood up, groaned, and stretched. "I should go for a run before dinner. You don't mind doing this?

"Why not? The files on the floor will still be here tomorrow."

While Liam ran, Aidan downloaded a zip file of all the messages, which dated back to about the time Edwin noticed Darius becoming preoccupied with something else. It was possible, of course, that Darius had found a Persian lover, and these were their billets-doux, but he doubted it.

While the zip file was downloading to Darius's laptop, Aidan retrieved his own and opened a translation app he had used in the past. Long ago, but not physically too far away, he'd been a teacher of English as a Second Language, working mostly with immigrants in Philadelphia at a variety of schools and colleges.

In the early 2000s, after a period of liberalism ended with a conservative return to power, a trickle of Iranian immigrants turned into a steady stream, and Aidan taught many liberal politicians and their families as they attempted to start new lives in the United States. He'd often used rudimentary translation apps to help him understand what they wanted to write about.

He had to download an update to the app, and by the time he finished that, and sent the zip file to his laptop, it was time to fix dinner. Liam returned and jumped into the shower, and Aidan grilled steaks and roasted tiny potatoes, which they had with a salad – served first, American style, for Edwin's comfort.

"Did you have a good nap?" Aidan asked Edwin, as they sat down to eat.

Edwin shrugged. "I dozed for a while. But it's hard to shut my brain off. I keep thinking of all the things I need to do." Edwin turned to Liam. "Do you speak to Aunt Doris much?"

"You know her. What do you think?"

Edwin laughed. "I understand. But Aunt Diane died two years ago, so Aunt Doris is my only blood aunt still alive. I talk to her once a month or so. Would you like to call her this evening?"

"No," Liam said forcefully. "Sorry, I didn't mean to say it like that. It's best that we focus on your problems and leave my mother for later."

"You should call her before you go back to France," Edwin said. "She speaks of you often."

"Really? Does she use the words fairy and faggot?"

Edwin looked down at the table. "She's been getting better. The money helps."

"What money?" Aidan asked.

"I've been sending her money now and then," Edwin said, looking up. "I have so much, and she and the girls need to be able to enjoy their lives."

"How much are you talking about?" Liam asked.

Edwin shrugged again. "The odd thousand now and then. When Francine broke up with Enzo again I sent her five, so she could get herself a new place."

Aidan looked at Liam, who appeared baffled. "So how much would you say you sent the three of them, last year, for example?" Liam asked.

"Oh, I don't keep close track," Edwin said, though Aidan didn't believe that. "Maybe, oh, twenty thousand or so?"

"You know you're enabling them," Liam said. "My sisters aren't stupid, just lazy. They could get jobs if they wanted."

"It's not that easy," Edwin said, and Aidan noticed that his posture had straightened. "Neither of your sisters have college degrees. The only jobs they're qualified for are low-skills ones like restaurant servers or hotel maids. And some of that money went for birthday and graduation gifts. When Andrea graduated from high school I paid for her to go the community college for their dental assistant program. And now she's working."

"My mother did say something about that," Liam said grudgingly.

"And you didn't think to ask where the money came from for that? You know your mother's living on your father's social security payments."

"She's never asked for anything."

"She's never had to ask you. She had my father and now me."

"Your father gave her money, too?" Liam asked.

Edwin stood up. "It's time you reevaluated your mother's life. It hasn't been easy, with a drunk for a husband, a son who ran out as soon as he could, and a pair of daughters who have even worse taste in men than she had."

He turned to Aidan. "Thank you for the dinner. I'm going to my room."

And then he left.

Chapter 10

Sophisticated

Liam

"Close your mouth, Liam," Aidan said. "You're letting in flies."

"Don't you start on me," Liam said. "The nerve of that asshole."

"You're hearing Doris's perspective on her life through his mouth," Aidan said. "And you know Doris is all about herself."

Liam closed his eyes and remembered. Money had always been tight in his house because Big Bill was a drunk. He never had a long-term job, and he blamed that on the bosses. They didn't appreciate him, and looked for any little excuse to fire him.

That's why he drank. That and his disappointment in his family, including his wife.

But what if Doris had been the one holding things together instead of causing the problems? When Liam thought back, they always had food on the table, and new clothes every fall. Cakes and gifts for their birthdays. Even special things like uniforms for sports or money for field trips.

Where had that money come from, if Big Bill was unemployed often and Doris didn't work outside the house? He'd never thought about that.

Aidan began to clear the table. "It isn't your fault," he said. "Whatever happened when you were a kid was up to your parents."

"I know," Liam said. "But maybe Edwin had a point."

Aidan turned to him. "You think we should send your mother money?"

Liam shook his head. "Edwin's got that taken care of."

"Then what?"

Liam stood up. "I don't know. Maybe cut her a little slack." He stretched his shoulders. "I need to go for another run. Work some stuff through in my head."

This time, he didn't worry about the security of Boca Largo. Instead, he put his head down and ran. It had been a mistake to take Edwin's phone call, and an even bigger one to come to Boca. He didn't owe the asshole anything, and they didn't need the money. They should have stayed in Banneret with their found family and left Edwin to his own devices.

But he couldn't help thinking about Big Bill and Doris and how he'd run away from them and their problems. Back then, he'd been in survival mode. He didn't know he was gay, exactly, but he knew that he didn't fit in with his family. He did his best in the gym, building his body so that he was bigger and stronger than his father, and when he graduated from high school and the Navy beckoned he took off.

He could count on the fingers of one hand the number of times he'd seen his family since then. Big Bill's funeral—he couldn't avoid that. Not just for his mother's sake, or his sisters, but for his own. He had to see the bastard put to rest.

A couple of other fly-by visits when he was on leave and

passing through the northeast. Then the visit ten years before, when he and Aidan had followed clients from Turkey to New Jersey. He'd wimped out on explaining his relationship with Aidan to his mother but then Aidan stepped up and told the truth and Doris had been a bitch.

He hadn't spoken to her for two years after that. Not until his sister Frannie had reached out because Doris had a cancer scare. It had been a false alarm, but he'd spoken to her, and they'd begun a regular series of calls a few times a year. Her birthday, and his, and Mother's Day and Christmas.

That was enough. Until now. Until Edwin's bombshell.

He finished a circuit of Boca Largo Drive and began another. He liked to think of himself as a good person, someone who had triumphed over a bad childhood to dedicate his life to taking care of other people. But in the process, he'd avoided his family of origin, leaving the caretaking up to Edwin Gallagher.

By the time he reached the house after two circuits, his muscles were singing and he was drenched in sweat. He went directly into the shower, then kissed Aidan good night and slid into bed. Maybe asleep he'd be able to shut off his brain.

When the burglar alarm went off at two in the morning, he was awake immediately. He shook Aidan's shoulder. "Someone's trying to break into the house," he said.

He jumped up and pulled on a pair of shorts. They hadn't been able to bring guns with them from France, but he had an expandable baton that he was able to get through security in his checked baggage. He grabbed it, grateful for the forethought that had him place it on the nightstand.

He picked up a flashlight from the same area, then opened the door silently. He crept forward in the dark, listening carefully, but all he heard was the alarm siren. By then Aidan was behind him, holding his own baton.

He'd long ago taught Aidan how to descend a staircase quietly, walking toe to heel. He placed the toe of his foot down first and slowly, then gently rolled his foot toward his heel, letting his body weight rest primarily over his back leg. He stayed close to the wall to avoid squeaks.

When he reached the first floor, Edwin was in the doorway to his bedroom, looking groggy. "That's the burglar alarm," he said.

"I got that," Liam said. "Go back in your room. Does the door have a lock?"

"It does."

"Lock yourself in. Lie down on the floor away from the window and wait for me or Aidan to come for you."

Edwin gulped, but he retreated into the room and closed the door. Liam heard the nick of the lock engaging.

Liam directed Aidan to go left, and he went right. In the kitchen, which faced the rear of the property, he spotted a window open by a couple of inches. Opening that window had tripped the magnetic sensor, and triggered the alarm. The sound had scared anyone away before they could get the window open wider and get into the house.

"You'd think they would have learned," Liam grumbled as Aidan joined him. "After the alarm went off for the back door before we got here."

"We don't know it was the same thief," Aidan said.

"True. Shut off the alarm off and get Edwin." He turned on the outside lights and went out to the backyard, which faced on a small lake. He walked around to the kitchen window, and spotted pry marks on it.

By then the alarm was off. He went back into the house as a police car pulled up on Gentle Rain Drive. He made sure that the two batons were stowed away so the police wouldn't see them.

Edwin met the two officers at the door and thanked them for coming out so quickly. Then he introduced Aidan and Liam, and Liam took them to the kitchen and showed them the marks.

"You wouldn't believe how many of these incidents we get in a month," the first officer said. "A lot of crooks out there who don't know how to recognize that there's an alarm system on the premises."

The second officer said, "Some of these houses were designed with a vertical window next to the door. All a crook has to do is look inside to see the lights on the alarm panel. Green means it hasn't been initiated and the house is fair game. Whoever set up this house avoided that problem."

They took down all the details. "We'll bump the report up to Detective Tseng and she'll contact you," the first officer said.

Edwin thanked them and they left. It was three o'clock in the morning, and he went back to his room.

Liam closed the kitchen window and made sure the alarm was registering it. Then he and Aidan went up to their room. "I'm worried about this," Liam said. "I can't help but believe that this break-in is tied to Darius's murder."

Aidan sat on the bed. "When I was a kid, my mother's aunts and uncles were starting to die off. I remember we'd go to the funeral, and then back to the person's house where the family was going to sit shiva—where they stay home for a few days and people come over to pay their condolences."

"And this matters because?" Liam asked, as he shucked the clothes he'd thrown on when he heard the alarm.

"My great-aunt had this friend, Syd Levy. She'd be the

one to stay at the house while everyone else was at the funeral. Because someone thought that crooks read the obituaries, and would break into the house while everyone was at the cemetery."

Liam cocked his head and looked at him.

"Maybe this is the same thing," Aidan continued. "Someone read about Darius in the paper. Saw that he was wealthy. Tracked down his address. Thought he'd break in and see what there was to steal."

"That's a possibility."

"Remember, this is Boca Raton," Aidan said. "I read somewhere that the average net worth of a household here is over $20 million. That would draw a lot of sophisticated thieves who would be on the lookout for opportunities."

"Then if these are smart thieves, why wouldn't they find a way to disable the alarm?"

Aidan yawned. "I don't know, Liam. But it's the middle of the night and I want to go back to sleep."

"And I want to talk to Detective Tseng tomorrow."

Chapter 11

Difficult Times

Aidan

Aidan, Liam, and Edwin talked over breakfast on Thursday morning about approaching Detective Tseng, but it didn't matter because she was on the doorstep as Aidan was clearing the table. Edwin ushered her into the living room and Liam joined them there. Aidan followed a moment later with a tray of coffee cups, creamer, and sugar.

"We were just finishing breakfast," Aidan said. "Can we offer you a coffee?"

"I'll never turn down caffeine," Tseng said, as she accepted a cup. "Thanks. I got the report of the break-in this morning and I wanted to come over and let you know that I'm considering the possibility that it might be related to Mr. Ashoori's murder."

"Thank you," Edwin said. "I'm getting more and more frightened."

To Aidan, Edwin looked tired, as if he hadn't been able to get back to sleep the night before – or maybe hadn't slept at all. He took a cup of coffee gratefully.

"Mr. Ashoori's shooting was in the local media. One of

my theories is that someone read about it including the details about the places he was shopping. They thought the house would be empty, and came looking for anything they could fence easily."

"What if it's more than that?" Edwin asked. "That whoever shot Darius was coming for me?"

"Do you have any information that would lead to that conclusion?" Tseng asked.

Aidan and Liam sipped their coffee while Edwin spoke. "We've been going through my husband's accounts. He sent a significant amount of money to an offshore account in the Cayman Islands."

"You didn't know about it?"

"I didn't. And I'm worried that whoever he was sending that money to wants more. From me."

She pulled a pad and pen from her jacket pocket and made notes. "Have you received any demands?"

"Not yet."

"If Mr. Ashoori was being blackmailed, it doesn't make sense that he'd be killed. You can't get money from a dead man." She looked at Edwin. "Unless there are terms in his will?"

"I haven't looked at it," Edwin said. "We had wills drawn up years ago that left everything to each other."

"Could he have changed his will recently? Say, when the money began flowing to the Caymans?"

"I'll have to call our attorney."

Aidan's heart went out to Edwin. He looked so defeated then.

Liam spoke first. "Can you check the security cameras for the community? See if they caught anyone coming in?"

"I will review the tapes," Tseng said. "But most of the camera setups in communities like this are more a deterrence than anything that generates evidence. Used to be, we worried about crooks jumping over a wall. But now they're more sophisticated."

She sipped the coffee for a moment. "These days one of the scams we're seeing is that criminals recruit Uber and Lyft drivers. When one of them has a legitimate delivery here, the crooks ride along, and while the driver's making his delivery, they do their thing, then meet up to ride out afterwards."

"Then the guard house will have a record of drivers, won't they?"

"They will, and we'll check it. But even the security guards here are savvy enough to question a delivery in the middle of the night, when your burglary was attempted. They must have had another way in that we don't know about."

She finished her coffee and put the cup and saucer down on the coffee table. Then she stood up. "Please contact me if the will indicates anything unusual. I'll let you know if we discover anything new."

Edwin rose and showed her out.

"That was a new idea," Aidan said. "About the will."

They waited until Edwin returned to the living room. "It's probably a good idea to call your lawyer this morning," Liam said. "On the off chance that Darius made a new will."

"Did he have any special bequests, that you recall?" Aidan asked. "Any family or friends?"

"His parents died years ago. He had a sister who remained in Tehran, who he argued with. She didn't understand that being a Jew would be difficult for her in an Islamic state." He shrugged. "She was arrested within a few years and died in prison. No children."

He turned to Liam. "So you see why it was important to me to keep in touch with Aunt Doris. I didn't want to lose touch with any of my family the way he did."

"I'm sorry I was angry yesterday," Liam said. "You made some points that I didn't want to face."

"It wasn't my intention to make you feel bad," Edwin said. "I hope you'll consider everything Aunt Doris had to face while you were growing up, and cut her some slack."

"That's easier said than done. But I'm working on it."

Aidan gathered the dirty coffee cups and took them into the kitchen. While he was cleaning up Liam joined him. "Edwin's going to call his attorney and look for the wills. He says they're in the safe in Darius's office."

"There's a safe? He might have mentioned that yesterday."

"Well, he mentioned it now," Liam said. "I'm going upstairs with him and then I'll go back to Darius's emails."

"I'll keep working on the files after I finish here."

Liam left, and Aidan loaded the dishwasher. It was more elaborate than any he'd ever seen before, with multiple cycles. He left it for Edwin to turn on and went upstairs, where he found Liam in the office.

"Because nothing is easy, Darius changed the combination on the safe at some point and didn't tell Edwin," Liam said. "He's going to call a locksmith."

"I don't like the way this is going," Aidan said, as he sat on the floor amidst the piles of paperwork. "Darius was keeping too many secrets."

"Secrets that probably got him killed," Liam said.

They worked in silence for an hour, until Liam said, "This is interesting."

Aidan looked up. "What's that?"

"Email receipts for a trip to Washington DC. About a week before the first payment went to the Caymans."

"Print that out so we can look at it later," Aidan said. After a minute, the printer began spitting out pages.

Edwin came into the office then. "Some good news," he said. "According to our attorney, Darius didn't create a new will with him. Though we don't know what's in the safe. The locksmith will be here this afternoon." He held up a piece of paper. "I bought the safe, so I have the paperwork establishing that I have the right to open it."

"That's good," Liam said. "Darius went to Washington a few months ago. Do you know why?"

"A friend of his, a diplomat in the State Department who handles Iran, was getting a commendation, and there was a ceremony. I am the president of our local choral society, and we had a concert and board meeting that conflicted, so I didn't go with him."

"Do you know this friend's name?" Liam asked. "I'd like to verify the ceremony if I can."

Edwin lost his balance, and Aidan jumped up to steady him as he began to cry. "It's all so much," he said. "First Darius dying, now every time I turn around I find something else he lied to me about, or might have lied about."

"These are difficult times," Aidan said. "You have every right to be sad, and angry, and whatever else you're feeling. But the important thing is that we learn everything we can about what Darius was doing so that we can protect you."

"Forty years," Edwin said through his tears. "I stood by that man for forty years. And all that time I thought he was there for me, too. What other lies are we going to find?"

He straightened up and wiped his eyes. "Harvey Grant," he said. "That's the man at the State Department."

Then he turned and walked out.

Chapter 12

Safecracker

Liam

After Edwin left Liam turned back to Darius's computer and searched for Harvey Grant at the State Department. He wasn't surprised to see that Grant had resigned from the government a year before under a cloud, making it unlikely that he was getting an award six months later. Not out of the realm of possibility, but another thing that Darius might have lied about.

He went back to the emails but hadn't found anything useful by the time Aidan stood up and said, "I'm going to fix lunch."

"I'll be down in a few minutes. I'm going to ask Richard to see what he can find out about this Harvey Grant." He composed an email and sent it off. Then he went downstairs, where Aidan was making cheesesteak sandwiches on the grill.

"My father used to make these for me," he was telling Edwin. "Not very gourmet, but he'd buy this thinly sliced beef and layer it with cheese and mushrooms. When I saw the same brand of beef at the grocery I couldn't resist buying it."

"Where did you grow up?" Edwin asked.

"The suburbs of Trenton. How about you?"

"Short Hills. Outside Newark."

"I know it," Aidan said. "A college friend was from there."

"A world away from New Brunswick," Liam said. "No wonder we didn't see you much growing up."

"My father was ashamed of Doris," Edwin said. "They came from the same background, but he pulled himself up and made money, and Doris married Bill and... well, you know."

"I don't remember anything about Doris's parents," Liam said. "They were both dead by the time I was old enough to notice."

"Our grandfather worked on the railroad," Edwin said. "He died when I was, oh, about ten or twelve. Then our grandmother came to live with us for a while, but she died a few years later. It's surprising how so many illnesses that were a death sentence back then are curable today. I couldn't even tell you what she died from. No one talked about it."

"That explains why I didn't know them," Liam said. It was strange to hear Edwin talk about 'our' grandparents, making the connection between them, when he'd hardly known the man until less than a week before.

He wasn't sure how he felt about that. He was so accustomed to his family being him, Aidan, and Hayam, with the addition of their found family around them on the Riviera. To realize that he had blood kin beyond his mother and sisters was taking some time to resolve.

Soon after they finished lunch, the locksmith arrived. He was a short, squat man named Anthony Colasanto. While Edwin showed him the appropriate paperwork,

Aidan cleared a space around the safe for Colasanto to work. "I do this all the time," he said. "People lose their combinations, or change them and forget them. It's not as easy as it looks in the movies, but it's doable."

Aidan and Edwin cleared out, leaving Liam with Colasanto. He opened his workbox and began to remove equipment. "This is an amplification device," he said. "Lots of different uses—leaks in pipes and so on. I connect the probe to the earphones and it makes it easier for me to hear the tumblers inside the lock. It can get the sound out from wood, brick, even armor plate."

He attached the probe to the door of the safe, inserted the earphones, and began turning the dials. Liam watched with interest. He'd never had to open a safe before, and probably never would again, but anything he could learn might be useful in the future.

It only took Colasanto about fifteen minutes before he sat back and opened the safe door. Liam summoned Edwin.

"That was quick," Edwin said.

"My father taught me everything," Colasanto said. "His parents brought him from Sicily to Buffalo when he was five years old, and by the time he was twelve he was working for a locksmith and learning the business. He always longed for the warm weather, and as soon as he could he moved to Florida and opened his own shop." He handed Edwin a card. "You need anything else, you call me."

"I will. Thank you." Edwin showed him out.

Liam sat on the floor in front of the opened safe. He began to remove paperwork and hand it to Aidan. "Deed to the house. Registration to the cars."

Edwin returned by then, and Aidan passed the papers to him. "I suppose I'll need this to sell the Rolls. I don't have any desire to keep it."

"That's what Darius was driving?" Aidan asked.

Edwin nodded. "Yet another thing I'll need to get back from the police. They still have it impounded for evidence."

"I'll make a note to ask Detective Tseng about the car when we talk to her next," Aidan said. "Maybe you can have the dealer pick it up from the police and buy it from you."

"Thank you."

Edwin took the next stack of papers from Liam and sat beside the safe, taking over Liam's role in emptying it. Liam moved to the desk chair. Aidan leaned against to the filing cabinet across from them.

"Here's my will," Edwin said. "That'll have to be changed now. I left everything to Darius, with some small bequests to Doris and her family and various charities."

He looked up at Liam. "You're part of that family."

"We're doing fine on our own," Liam said. "I'm sure there are charities that could use the money more than we could."

"And we hope you live a long, happy life," Aidan added.

Edwin turned to a manila folder and opened it. Many pages were attached inside by a clip along the top. "Now we're getting somewhere," Edwin said. "This is Darius's will."

He began scanning through the pages. "The same, the same... Oh, what's this? The Organization for a Democratic Persia?"

Liam turned to Darius's computer and did a quick search. "According to Wikipedia, it's a loosely-based umbrella group of those who are opposed to the Iran's Islamic Republic government. Their goal is to replace the mullahs with a democratically elected leadership."

He looked at Edwin. "You never heard of them?"

Edwin shook his head. "I tuned out when Darius started talking about Persia. I guess I should have listened more carefully."

"And this group wasn't in his initial will?"

Edwin quickly flipped through the pages. "No, here's the original will, and no mention of them."

"You said your attorney didn't know about a new will," Aidan said.

"This is a codicil," Edwin said. "An addition to the will. Signed by Darius, and witnessed by two people I've never heard of. Diego Cruz and Elena Santiago." He looked closely at the document. "This was signed and witnessed in Washington, D.C., when Darius was there to see Harvey Grant."

"Those don't sound like Persian names," Liam said. "Maybe they were staff at the hotel where Darius was staying."

"How much did Darius leave the ODP?" Aidan asked.

"The Fidelity account is to be transferred to them," Edwin said. "Whatever is left there of the six point something million he opened the account with."

"Does that give someone in that group an incentive to kill Darius?" Aidan asked. "To accelerate the funding? Maybe they need the money quicker than Darius was willing to give it to them."

"Hold on," Liam said. While he loved Aidan's ability to think outside the box that Liam's training put him in, his husband often engaged in flights of fancy that had little backing. "First of all, we don't know that the ODP is behind the Cayman Islands account. The Caymans have very strict bank privacy laws, and Richard can't establish who owns the account. And even if they are, if Darius was parceling the money out to them on a regular basis, why kill him? It takes time to settle an estate, so they're going to have to wait longer for the money. And we have no evidence to indicate that they wanted it faster."

"Until we get those emails translated," Aidan said. "I'll check on the progress the app is making." He turned back to Edwin. "Anything else in there?"

"This," Edwin said, holding up a key. "I recognize the pattern of the teeth on it. My father had a key a lot like this one that went to a safe deposit box at his bank. The thing is, I didn't know Darius and I had a box."

Chapter 13

Key

Aidan

"There's probably a receipt somewhere in Darius's files," Aidan said. "I've been looking through all of them but I haven't found anything from a bank yet."

"Is there any marking on the key?" Liam asked.

Edwin peered at the key. "There's a tag with a nine-digit number on it. Hold on a second."

He pulled out his wallet and extracted a blank check from inside it. "I think this is a bank routing number. It matches the format. Four digits for the Federal Reserve and four for the bank, with a check digit at the end. But it doesn't match the one for Chase, which is the bank we use."

He read it off to Liam, who searched for a match online. "Got it. Founder's First Bank, headquartered in DC. Only five branches in the district, Maryland, and Virginia."

"That makes sense," Aidan said. "If Darius was in Washington and wanted to use a small private bank."

"What do you know about Darius's trip there?" Liam asked. "You said it was for his friend Harvey Grant to get an award, but Grant had left the State Department under questionable circumstances. People who leave like that don't get awards."

Edwin put his head in his hands, and his shoulders shook. "Is there anything Darius told me that I can believe?" He looked up, and Aidan saw tears at the edges of his eyes. "At the time, he said that he was sorry that the event for Harvey conflicted with my choral society obligations. But now I wonder if he deliberately scheduled that trip so that I couldn't go with him."

"The timing of the trip is suspicious," Liam said. "Everything we've seen seems to have started after that. That's when he began hiding things from you, when he started the new Proton Mail email account, and when the disbursements from the Fidelity Account began."

"I wish I could tell you more," Edwin said. "But I was so busy with my own affairs that I never asked him much about the trip. He flew up, said he went to the ceremony, and then came home."

He shook his head. "I need a nap before dinner." He stood, using the edge of the desk to keep his balance, and left the room.

Aidan watched him go with concern. "This is all taking a toll on Edwin."

"I understand," Liam said. "But we can't let any detail go until we figure out what Darius was doing, and if that has any bearing on why he was killed."

"And if a threat still remains to Edwin." Aidan grabbed his laptop from the desk and slid down to the floor. "I'll see if the Proton Mail messages have been decoded yet."

Liam went back to the computer. "While you do that, I'll dig through Darius's credit card receipts from that trip. Maybe they'll tell us something."

Aidan opened his laptop and engaged the translation

app. Darius had sent about a dozen messages to a single email address, also on Proton Mail. Aidan had been able to retrieve all those, as well as the address they were sent to, and receipts that indicated they had been read. But because incoming messages had been sent from an encrypted account, he couldn't view them.

He read through the outgoing ones. The grammar was awkward; the translation app wasn't perfect at converting Farsi to the English. If necessary, they could hire an experienced translator, but as Aidan read, he realized that wouldn't be necessary. Most of the messages were along the lines of "I sent you the money."

That wasn't particularly useful, and Aidan wondered why Darius had gone to the trouble of setting up a separate account. So that Edwin wouldn't realize what was going on? Or was he worried that someone was spying on his regular account?

Aidan sat back and looked up at Liam. "I've got nothing." He explained the messages he'd been able to review. "Raises more questions than answers."

"Our friend Darius was up to something, that's for sure," Liam said. "I haven't been to DC in a long time, but if I was going to an event near the State Department offices in the Truman Building on C Street, I'd stay nearby. There are lots of luxury hotels where a guy like Darius could feel pampered. But instead he stayed at the Holiday Inn Express."

"Really?"

"That's where I have a receipt for. Two nights. And he didn't eat at anywhere fancy, either. Receipts from local delis and pizza parlors."

"Sounds like he didn't want to be recognized anywhere," Aidan said.

"That's my feeling."

Aidan leaned back against the filing cabinet. "Let's recap. About six months ago, Darius flew to DC for a meeting he kept secret from Edwin. His hotel and meals are out of keeping with his normal luxury. After that, he opened the Fidelity account and started sending money to this Iranian foundation. He changed his will without telling Edwin, and he stored a key to a bank deposit box in his safe."

"Get on to Richard when you can," Liam said. "Have him see what he can dig up on this group, and if he's made any progress on my request for information on Harvey Grant."

Aidan sent the message to Richard, and then continued searching through Darius's paper receipts. So far, all he'd found were legitimate purchases of antiques and décor, with provenance for anything old.

As the light faded, Aidan abandoned his search and went into the kitchen to prepare dinner. This was getting to be routine, which was dangerous. How long would they have to stay with Edwin? And at what point would they start letting their guard down?

He was preoccupied with his thoughts, and with figuring out what to make for dinner, that he didn't notice Edwin come into the kitchen until he spoke. "I settled one thing," he said.

"What's that?"

"Detective Tseng has released Darius's Rolls. I called the dealer and arranged for them to pick it up and give me a quote to purchase it. I'm sure they'll low-ball it but I don't care. I never want to see that car again."

Aidan was a bit disappointed, because he'd been hoping

to ride in the Rolls at least once, but he understood Edwin's position.

"That's good progress," Aidan said. "Now that the funeral home has Darius's body, you should be able to get copies of the death certificate from them. Do you think you might be up for a quick trip to DC after the funeral? Someone is going to have to arrive in person at the bank with the key, and it's easier if it's you."

"So many details," Edwin said. "I never imagined having to do all this so soon. Darius was a few years older than I was, but I thought we'd have another ten or twenty years together."

"I'm sorry," Aidan said. "It's something I face periodically with Liam. Our business puts us in danger and I worry that he'll get hurt, or killed."

"How do you deal with that?"

"Willful denial," Aidan said with a smile. "But more important, we try and make every day count. If we argue, we make up quickly. We keep our focus on safety and avoid big risks."

"And you're honest with each other?"

"I hope so. We both believe in that." He gave up looking through the kitchen cabinets. "Any idea what you'd like for dinner?"

"Can we order in? Would that be safe? Darius's favorite food was sushi, but mine has always been pizza. There's a great pizzeria not too far from here that delivers."

"Sounds like a great idea. But I'll confirm with Liam first."

"Communication," Edwin said. "Something that was apparently very lacking in my relationship with Darius."

Chapter 14

Lies

Liam

Liam agreed to pizza, and when the delivery arrived, he stepped outside to receive it from an older Italian man who wished him *Buon Appetito*.

As they sat at the kitchen table, the rich aroma of the sausage, mushrooms, and tomatoes rising around them, he asked Edwin what he knew about Harvey Grant.

"Darius had a deep and abiding interest in his homeland," Edwin said. "We met Harvey at an event in Manhattan about ten years ago, as we were negotiating the sale of the business. He and Darius clicked, and they spoke periodically. At least twice, Harvey came to Florida on either business or vacation and he and Darius got together."

"Any idea what they talked about?"

"Well, Darius was a royalist, and he thought the best way forward for Iran was to reinstate the shah, in the person of the younger Reza Pahlavi. Harvey was more of a pragmatist, a sounding board. He wasn't sure the people of Iran wanted the shah back, and he was leaning toward a democratic government."

"Is that a realistic hope?" Liam asked.

Edwin shrugged. "I left the politics to them. I was surprised when you told me that Harvey was no longer at the State Department—the way Darius talked about him he was still very involved in the future of Iran."

"Which he might have been," Liam said. "Perhaps that involvement is why he had to leave his job."

"Tell me something personal about Grant," Aidan said. "Gay? Straight?"

"Straight. Married to the same woman for decades. Lovely lady. Her father was a general, and Harvey met her when he was at West Point. He was determined to make a career in the Army, but after he did his time in the Gulf War, his father-in-law got him a job in the State Department. He had a knack for those Middle Eastern languages—Arabic, Farsi, Pashto, and Dari. It's my impression—just a guess—that he was attached to the CIA at some point. I know he spent some time in Afghanistan."

"Sounds like an interesting guy," Aidan said.

"He was also an Orientalist, if you can use that term today. Fascinated by the history of the area and the antiquities Darius collected. He had a few pieces of his own, picked up on his travels. He sold Darius one of those spice bottles in the cabinet."

Liam took the pizza box out to the recycle bin and stood in the house's side yard for a moment, looking up at the stars. He saw more of them in Banneret because there was so much less ground light in the country than there was in Boca. But he made out the north star, and the three stars in Orion's belt, and that gave him some comfort.

It was quieter in Banneret, too. As he stood there, he heard the low rumble of air conditioning compressors, the squeal of tires as someone took a corner too quickly. In the far distance he heard a siren—police or fire on their way to someone else's bad day.

He went back inside, and he and Aidan retired to their room. "Message from Richard," Aidan said, as he scanned his laptop. "Mostly background on the shah's widow and their son. But here's something interesting."

"What's that?"

"Richard found regular email correspondence between Darius and the Shahbanu up until about six months ago. Then nothing."

"That would be about the time of his visit to DC," Liam said. "Did he meet with her then?"

"Nothing to indicate that. But she does mention that her son is looking forward to seeing him soon."

"How about messages with the son?" Liam asked.

"They agree to a meeting when he's in DC, but nothing after that."

"You think they had a disagreement?"

Aidan shrugged. "Could be. Something had to happen to stop the connection between them."

"I wonder if Harvey Grant had anything to do with that."

"Grant's next on Richard's list."

Liam did a thorough check of the house before they went to bed, making sure that all the windows and doors were armed. It was clear to him that an unknown person wanted Edwin, the key to the safe deposit box, or something else.

Friday morning dawned gray and cloudy—not what he expected of Florida. The temperature had dropped ten degrees overnight, and big-bellied gray clouds hung low over Boca Largo. He stood outside Edwin's front door and stretched, then took off at an easy trot down Gentle Rain Drive.

A restless wind ruffled the tops of the palm trees and squirrels chased each other up and down the rough trunks. As he turned onto Boca Largo Promenade, he passed one of the security guards in a small SUV with the name of the company plastered on the side. He watched as the woman inside pulled over in front of a house, then got out. She aimed her cell phone at a tree, then got back in her car and drove away.

After she was gone, Liam stopped by the tree and spotted a small sensor tapped into the trunk. Interesting. The guards probably had a prescribed route, and checking in with those sensors proved they were doing their job. Now if they'd only been able to prevent the attempted break-in at the house on Wednesday night.

As he circled along the Promenade, a six-foot electric-green iguana slithered across the road and down along the bank of one of the small lakes. It disappeared into a hole. A mourning dove, its feathers light brown with black specks, landed on the branch of an oak and cooed.

Liam saluted it, then sped up as thunder cracked so loud that it startled him. The wind picked up, and with it the rain. It had turned into a downpour by the time he reached Gentle Rain Drive. "Gentle rain my ass," he said as he ducked inside.

Aidan was waiting with a fluffy bath sheet for him. He dried off and then followed his husband to the kitchen. Over breakfast, Liam watched the storm raged outside, through the kitchen window.

Wind tossed the tops of the palm trees and splattered the windows. The phrase "not a fit day for man or beast" popped into his head as he ate. He wondered how Hayam was getting along without them. Probably being spoiled rotten by Thierry and Slava.

He'd never had a pet growing up. Doris refused to have another mouth to feed, and he had to agree she was probably right. Then when he was in the Navy he'd traveled so much he couldn't have had a dog or cat if he'd wanted one.

When he landed in Tunis, he was lonely, and thought about getting a pet. One of the men who hung around the Bar Mamounia had a parrot he kept on his shoulder, and his back was often splattered with trails of white poop. That soured him on birds. Occasionally he'd see a stray dog on the street and try to befriend it, but they were often too wary.

Then he'd met Aidan, and seen his connection to the little lion-faced dog. When Aidan moved in with him, the dog came along, and it took a couple of months before Liam felt Hayam had accepted him as her second daddy.

Now she would curl up with him when he sat on the sofa to read or play video games, and he loved the feeling of her warm body next to his leg. He was getting soft, he knew. That hard-edged SEAL he'd once been had been tamed and civilized by life with Aidan, and he never wanted to go back.

As he was clearing the table, Aidan suggested that Edwin contact Harvey Grant. "He might not know that Darius was killed," he said. "You could pass that information to him and see how he responds. Ask him if he knows any reason someone could come after Darius."

"I doubt he'd say anything, but I can call," Edwin said. "But I'd need Darius's phone. Harvey's number is in there, and I think he'd answer a call from Darius."

"The police haven't returned that to you yet?" Liam asked.

"It could be in the bags that Detective Tseng brought over the other day," Aidan said.

Liam turned to Edwin. "Can we look through the bags, and the phone, before you make the call? On the off chance there's something interesting."

"Be my guest."

By then the rain had passed, leaving only glittering puddles in the driveway. Liam went into the garage through the kitchen door. It was a big space, the floor covered in tile. Aidan had parked their rented SUV next to a dark green Alfa Romeo Stelvio SUV, Edwin's ride. He found a group of three plastic bags on a shelf along one side of the garage, and a quick look revealed they contained the bags Darius had bought at the Town Center.

He carried them all into the kitchen, and while Edwin waited in the living room he and Aidan sorted through the contents. A man's leather belt from Louis Vuitton and a set of decorative plates from Versace. A bottle of Gucci Guilty Pour Homme, eau de toilette.

Darius's wallet, phone, and a key chain with another fob in the shape of Iran. This had a series of keys on it, including an electric key with the distinctive RR logo. Liam recognized the key to the front door, and put aside the others to examine later.

He carried the phone out to the living room. "We found his phone, but it needs a charge."

"There's a cord plugged into the wall over there," Edwin said.

Liam plugged it in and watched the phone come back to life. When it did, Edwin picked it up, still attached to the cord. "Do you want me to put him on speaker?" he asked.

"Let's not let on that you've hired us," Liam said. "We'll stay close to you."

The phone needed face activation or a code. "Darius was consistent with his passwords. Try 0901," Edwin said, and that worked to unlock the phone.

Liam scanned through the missed calls first. Two from Edwin, and one from a doctor's office. He skipped to the Contacts screen and found Harvey's number.

"Here you go," he said, and he handed the phone to Edwin. He sat to his cousin's left, and Aidan joined them to Edwin's right.

His hand shaking, Edwin pushed the button on the phone to dial Harvey.

"This must be Edwin," a man's voice said after two rings. It was loud enough that they could all hear without engaging the speaker.

"It is," Edwin said. "So you know about Darius."

"I have alerts set up for many people I know," Harvey said. "I'm so sorry about Darius. I should have called to offer my condolences, but I realized I didn't have your number and I didn't know if you'd have access to Darius's phone."

"The police just gave it back to me." Edwin hesitated. "I have to ask, Harvey. Do you know any reason why someone would want to kill my husband?"

"I thought it was a robbery," Harvey said. "That's what I read in the paper, at least. I've often told Darius he was too flashy. At least swap out the gold and diamond Rolex for a Patek Philippe or a Vacheron Constantin. They're harder for thieves to recognize."

"You know he loved his labels," Edwin said. "But I don't think it was a robbery attempt, though that's what the police say. I'm discovering that Darius was keeping a lot of secrets from me."

"Really? What kind?"

"Do you know anything about the Organization for a

Democratic Persia? Darius had been sending them money every month."

"He was a soft touch for anything to do with Persia," Harvey said. "You know that."

Liam rolled his finger in a circular motion, hoping Edwin would realize he wanted him to pursue that, and he did.

"What do you know about that organization?" Edwin asked.

"One of a loose coalition of groups that want to remove the chokehold the mullahs have on Iran," Harvey said.

Edwin leaned forward. "Connected to Reza Pahlavi?"

"No, they believe that the people don't want the monarchy returned. That they want democracy."

"That seems an unlikely cause for Darius to support, given how close he was to the Shahbanu."

"People change their minds," Harvey said. "Darius was smart enough to see the wind changing direction. Do you know if Darius had a will?"

Out of the corner of his eye, Liam spotted one of the many photos of Darius with the Shah's widow. If he'd changed his opinion he hadn't revised his décor.

"I'm looking into it," Edwin said. "One more thing. Darius went to Washington a few months ago. He said you were getting an award from the State Department. Congratulations on that."

"Thank you. It was kind of him to show up. Anyway, I've got a meeting to get to. Let me know if there's anything I can do for you."

Harvey ended the call.

"Interesting question about the will," Aidan said. "I wonder if Darius told Harvey how much he was giving that group. And if he was going to fulfill a pledge to them."

"I bet Harvey knew exactly how much Darius was giving, and what the conditions were," Liam said. "And I'll bet that Richard is going to dig up a connection between Harvey and that group."

"And he lied about the award," Edwin said. "We already knew there was no award and that he'd left the State Department. I wonder why he didn't say something about that."

"Because that would have opened up a new line of questions he didn't want to answer." Liam stood. "I'm going back up to the office."

Chapter 15

Connections

Aidan

When Liam left, Aidan turned to Edwin. "What would you like us to do with the things Darius bought at the mall? Put them back in the garage?"

"Can you add them to the pile we're giving away? And do you think it would be safe to go out this afternoon and deliver those bags we packed? I'd like to get them out of the house."

"I'll check with Liam." He put his hand on Edwin's shoulder. "I know this is tough, but you're getting through it."

Edwin put his hand over Aidan's. "Thank you. Having you and Liam here is a big help."

Aidan went upstairs to finish looking through Darius's receipts. He'd already sorted most of them, the household expenses separated from the artifacts. He sat on the floor while Liam worked at the desk. After another half hour, he was finished.

"I can't find any evidence that Darius was buying things illegally. I've put everything that relates to the collectibles in one pile, so that if Edwin wants to sell anything, he'll have the provenance easily at hand."

Liam pivoted in his chair to face Aidan. "What do you think he's going to do?"

"I don't know. And I don't think he does either. If I were him, I'd stay in Boca, where he has friends and connections. But I might sell this house and move somewhere for a fresh start."

"I'd be as lost as he is," Liam said. "If anything happened to you."

"You'd manage. We have a found family back in Banneret."

Liam shook his head. "It's not about that. Our lives are so connected. I rely on you."

"I love you, too," Aidan said. "I admit, I've been thinking about it myself. That time you fell off the ladder? I was so scared of losing you. But the fact is that one of us is going to go before the other, and one of us will have to go on alone. I was talking about this with Edwin, and I said that you and I both work on being present for each other. Not keeping secrets, not getting angry."

"We get angry. But we make up afterwards."

"I agree. We know life is precious and neither of us wants to waste a minute of it."

Liam sighed. "Well, we still have work to do here. I've identified a couple of email accounts for further investigation. If you come over here, we could do some preliminary work together. You still work the computer better than I do."

"Agreed," Aidan said with a smile. He stood and pushed the visitor's chair around beside Liam. "Scoot over. Who's the first person?"

"How about this guy? Parviz Esfahani. That's about as Persian as you can get."

Aidan took over the keyboard and typed in the name. The first link went to a page on LinkedIn, and he clicked there. "Graduate student at the University of Miami," he read. "Specialist in Middle Eastern History. Available for consultation work with regard to tribal claims and oil and gas contracts. And here's a link to his blog."

He clicked through. "Persia, Persia, Persia," he said, as he scanned through the titles of posts. He looked at Liam. "What's in his emails to Darius?"

"Mostly times and places to meet," Liam said. "Occasional questions about the translation of a complex word or phrase from Farsi."

They followed a few more links but couldn't find anything else of interest about Esfahani. Another half-dozen of the names linked to people from Darius's work in fashion, often comments about a problem with a company or a supplier, or snide comments about someone's work.

The remaining names were all Boca residents. One man was eager to recruit Darius to his pickleball league, while another coordinated times when they met to swim together at a health club with an Olympic-sized pool.

"Edwin wants to get rid of the things he packed up from Darius's closet," Aidan said. "He asked if we could go out this afternoon."

"In general I'd rather keep him here, where he's safest," Liam said. "But we both know that clients get itchy when they're cooped up. So see where he wants to go and how safe the area is."

Aidan went downstairs, where Edwin was on the phone. "Thanks for calling," he said. "I appreciate it. And I'll try to make the meeting next week."

He ended the call. "One of the board members from the opera fund," he said. "Gradually people are reaching out to me, which is nice. I feel like I have a way to move forward."

"Liam says it's okay to head out to the thrift store, depending on where it is."

"Darius liked the one at the Jewish Community Center," he said. "They'd do better with his clothes than Goodwill. It's not far—a few blocks off Glades Road on the other side of I-95."

Aidan called up a map on his phone. The area looked safe enough, sandwiched between a university campus and the Intracoastal Waterway.

"There's one more thing we should do while we're out," Aidan said. "Take the suit and the other clothes over to the funeral home."

"Can you take care of that? I don't even want to go into the building."

"What about the casket? Jews usually go for simple ones."

Edwin shook his head. "Darius wasn't that observant. Pick out the most expensive one—that's what he would want."

"And the service? Don't you want to have input there?"

"No. No viewing or open casket. Just a graveside service."

Aidan left Edwin downstairs and went up to Darius's bedroom. He put the suit into a hanging bag and packed the rest of the clothes neatly into an old suitcase. On his way down to the car, he stopped at the office. Liam was wearing his reading glasses again, looking closely at the screen, but he whipped the glasses off quickly as if embarrassed by them.

"What's up?" he asked.

Aidan held up what he was carrying. "We need to deliver these to the funeral home. I checked out the thrift store where Edwin wants to drop off his donations, and the area looks safe. Are you ready to leave?"

Liam pushed back from the desk. "I would love to get out from behind this desk."

He and Liam loaded everything into the hatch of the rented SUV, and then Edwin slid into the back seat. Aidan's phone app provided directions to the thrift shop, and they drove there in silence.

The thrift shop was in what Aidan was coming to expect as a typical South Florida strip center, with beige stucco and Mediterranean accents. He parked in front and said, "I can take care of this."

"Leave the air conditioning on," Liam said, as he pulled out his phone.

It took Aidan three trips to get all the bags into the thrift shop. "Don't let the method of delivery turn you off," he said to the clerk. "Lots of designer clothes in great condition."

"Excellent, thank you," the clerk said. Aidan received a receipt for tax purposes and then returned to the SUV.

"Next stop the funeral home," Aidan said, as he slid behind the wheel. He followed directions a few miles south on Dixie Highway to a two-story building adjacent to a synagogue. He carried the remaining bags inside, and was directed to a consultant's office.

Sylvia Fein was a motherly woman in her mid-fifties. Aidan introduced himself. "I'm the one who spoke to you on the phone," he said. "Mr. Ashoori's husband is my husband's cousin. Mr. McCullough isn't up to having this conversation, and since I'm Jewish and he isn't, I volunteered to take care of things for him."

She nodded. "Saying goodbye can be very painful." She turned to her computer and brought up Darius's file. "Thank you for bringing in Mr. Ashoori's clothes. There are a few things we still need to handle. Did you want to purchase a vault in the mausoleum or a cemetery plot?"

"Cemetery plot. And as I said, we'll have graveside services."

She pushed back her chair. "Let me show you the caskets we have available."

She led him into a showroom, but after spending a few days in Darius's house, Aidan knew immediately which one he'd want. The Elite Cherry with cream velvet interior. The wood was glossy and the accessories tasteful. A star of David had been incised into the top.

They went back to Sylvia's office and handled the remaining details. Darius's body would be transported to the cemetery on Sunday morning. "Will you have pall bearers?" she asked.

"I don't think so. Mr. Ashoori didn't have a lot of family."

"If you or Mr. McCullough wish, we can designate honorary pallbearers to accompany Mr. Ashoori from the hearse to the grave."

Aidan shivered. But who knew? Perhaps many of Darius's friends would show up and accept the honor.

A rabbi would join them at the grave to say the requisite prayers. There were various additional charges. "We'll put up a temporary marker," Sylvia said. "Then at his convenience Mr. McCullough can choose a headstone design. Do you know if he wants to purchase the adjoining plot?"

Thinking of all the secrets Darius had been keeping, Aidan said, "This isn't a good time to raise that question.

Can you put a hold on selling it to someone else for a while?"

"We can do that," Sylvia said. "But not for an unlimited period of time."

"I understand." Aidan pulled out Edwin's credit card to cover the interment and recording fees. He inserted it into the electronic machine then scrawled a signature. He rose and thanked Sylvia for her help.

"I consider this job a mitzvah," she said. "And what you're doing is a mitzvah as well."

He smiled, shook her hand, and then walked back out to the SUV. "All done," he said as he got back in. "Do we head for home now?"

Edwin asked, "Could we go for a drive? Not go back to the house right away?"

"Where did you want to go?" Liam asked.

"Up along the water?" Edwin asked. "A1A is very pretty between here and Palm Beach. And Darius loved being by the ocean."

Liam looked over at Aidan. "Make it so."

Aidan smiled. "Geek," he said.

Aidan glanced at the map on his phone, then headed east on Palmetto Park Road. "It's really pretty here," he said as they drove. "What made you guys want to move to Florida?"

"We knew people here, so it was an easy transition," Edwin said. "Boca Largo was under construction, so we bought the land and had the house built to our specifications. And then we got involved in various charities, and you know, time passed."

Aidan looked over at Liam. He knew how that happened. They had been in Banneret for nearly twelve years, and yet it seemed like only a moment ago that they'd been in Tunis, in the little house behind the Bar Mamounia.

Palmetto Park Road was lined with strip shopping centers, churches, and the entrances to more gated communities. When they reached A1A, Aidan took a deep breath. The blue-green ocean was entrancing, sails puffed above boats moving south for the winter, and the occasional whitecaps danced along the shore.

The road was lined with high-rises to the right and more gated communities to the left. Liam leaned over to Aidan and said, "I haven't noticed anyone following us. Want to suggest lunch?"

"Sure." He asked Edwin, who said there were a lot of nice places along Atlantic Avenue in downtown Delray Beach.

The barrier island that separated the mainland from the ocean was narrow there, and they caught glimpses of the Intracoastal to their left as they headed north. "So much money," Aidan said. "I can't imagine what it costs to live in one of these towers by the ocean."

"Some of them are older," Edwin said. "People bought in decades ago. But you're right, there is a lot of money down here."

Aidan was happy with the life he shared with Liam. They lived on the French Riviera, after all, though miles inland from the ocean. They had good weather for most of the year, excellent friends around them, and the French culture that led to a relaxed lifestyle. But he couldn't help imagining what it would be like to be rich.

Not billionaire level, of course. That kind of money carried its own problems. And it was still possible that Darius's wealth had led to his death. But maybe enough to live in one of those towers with the ocean stretching out.

Being a patron of the arts like Edwin. Never having to risk his life, or his husband's, again.

That wasn't happening. He knew they would have to get out of close protection someday—their bodies wouldn't hold up, or their minds wouldn't be sharp enough. With luck, they'd have new plans in place by the time they needed them.

"Turn left at the next light," Edwin said from the back seat. "That's Atlantic Avenue. Park wherever you can find a space. There are a lot of restaurants to choose from."

Aidan found a space across from a waterfront restaurant by the Intracoastal, and they were escorted to an outdoor table with a view of small boat traffic heading north and south.

"I'm glad we're getting to know each other," Edwin said to Liam after they'd ordered. "You've always been an indistinct branch on the family tree but I knew from Aunt Doris that you were gay and I thought we might have something in common."

"We grew up very differently," Liam said.

"But there's a blood connection," Edwin said. "Do you feel it at all?"

Aidan looked over at Liam, curious to hear what he'd say. "I do," Liam said eventually. "I don't understand it, but yes, there's something there."

"It's probably partly what draws me and Liam together," Aidan said. "We're all Jersey boys. And growing up in the Garden State gives you a particular experience. I may be from Trenton and Liam from New Brunswick and you from Short Hills, but there's something we shared."

"I like hearing about our grandparents," Liam said. "I never really knew them."

"I have a few stories, if you'd like."

"Yes, please."

The meal passed easily, as Edwin told about quirky things their grandmother had said, the way she would only have a half a cup of coffee after dinner, the way she liked to have her arm twisted to eat a second piece of Danish pastry. He retold stories their grandfather had shared about his work on the railroad.

By the end of the meal, Aidan felt like he knew them. And he was glad that Liam was getting to know his cousin, too. Funny how things worked out like that.

It was late afternoon by the time they returned to Boca Largo. Edwin had some calls to make, and Liam and Aidan went up to their room where a new report from Richard had come in.

Aidan sat on the edge of the bed while Liam took a chair at the desk against the wall. They each read through it on their respective laptops. When he finished reading the report, Aidan clicked through to the spreadsheet Richard had retrieved from Grant's bank account. He didn't even want to think about how their hacker had gotten it, but it showed interesting patterns. Large deposits, anywhere from ten to fifty thousand dollars, over the past year.

He clicked back to the statements from Darius's Fidelity account and compared them to Grant's. Each time Darius sent a hundred thousand dollars to the Cayman Islands account, twenty-five thousand dollars appeared in Grant's account.

Aidan waited until Liam had finished reading Richard's report. "As we expected, Harvey Grant is a lot more connected to the group Darius has been donating to than he let on," he said.

"Being on the board is a pretty big connection," Liam said. "Though sometimes the board members are figureheads. Former politicians or people with connections for fund-raising."

"It's more than that," Aidan said. He explained about the money Grant was skimming from each of Darius's donations. "And he's probably doing that with other rich donors as well." He shifted his laptop so Liam could see Grant's bank statement.

Liam nodded. "You don't make a fortune working for the government, or at least that's what Louis says. And Grant is getting older and I'm sure he's thinking about the future."

"There are a lot of payments to a Medipol University Hospital in Istanbul," Aidan said. "Maybe Grant is sick and needs the money to pay medical bills."

"It's not Grant," Liam said. "Look back at Richard's report. It's his wife. She has a brain tumor, and she's getting a lot of expensive experimental treatments that aren't covered by insurance."

"Why didn't he just ask Darius for the money?" Aidan asked. "Why go through this elaborate subterfuge?"

"Brain tumors are fatal nearly seventy percent of the time," Liam said. "A buddy of mine in the SEALs had one, and he was dead within six months. Of course there are all kinds of tumors, some easier to treat than others."

"So Grant could be looking to his future as a single man, too," Aidan said. He pulled up a photo of the man from his State Department time. "Good looking, in a silver fox way. With enough money, he could attract a younger beauty and kick-start his life."

"You're spinning a story again," Liam said. "We don't have enough information to know what his motives are."

"Agreed." Aidan sat back in his chair. "What do you think about the other organizations that Richard dug up?"

"There's an interesting range," Liam said. "The ODP is the most liberal, democratic one. Then there's the Iranian Religious Force. They're backed by the mullahs, and willing to use intimidation and pressure to enforce religious law. Richard also says that many of the current politicians in Iran come from a military background, and they're more interested in trade, economy and infrastructure than in religious rhetoric. They have connections to at least one or two of the groups in the US."

"Do you think one of them could be behind Darius's death?" Aidan asked. "If the IDF or a group backed by Iranian politicians knew he was funding their opposition, they'd have a strong motive to kill him and shut off that pipeline."

"If Grant didn't know what's in Darius's will, then it's likely the mullahs behind the IDF and the military politicians don't either."

"If someone from the IDF killed Darius, then who tried to break into the house on Wednesday night?" Liam asked.

Aidan shrugged. "Could be random thieves who read about Darius on the news. Or maybe Darius left something behind that they want."

"Something in the safe deposit box?" Liam asked.

Aidan shrugged. "It all goes back to March, when Darius went to DC."

"We need to go back further," Liam said. "The last communication between Darius and Reza Pahlavi was in February. From what I read, Darius was frustrated with Pahlavi's progress on getting back to the Peacock Throne."

Aidan nodded. "I got that too. Pahlavi sounded pragmatic. That a whole lot of events had to come together, starting with on-the-ground protests in Iran. He said he saw progress, but it was going to take more time."

"Then there's the unsent response I found in Darius's digital trash," Liam said. "He said that he wanted to see progress and was willing to pay for it. Instead of sending it though, he contacted Harvey Grant to ask him if he could put pressure on Pahlavi through diplomatic channels."

Aidan nodded. "And Grant responded that Darius should look into the Organization for a Democratic Persia. Darius made plans to fly up to DC and meet with Grant."

"That's where the lies begin," Liam said. "He didn't tell Edwin the truth. Why not?"

"Maybe because Edwin wouldn't approve? Six million dollars is a lot of money. And Edwin didn't have the same emotional connection with Iran that Darius did."

"It was Darius's business that generated the money. He probably believed he could decide what to do with it."

"And he wasn't leaving Edwin destitute."

Liam nodded. "So Darius flew to DC, met with Harvey, and agreed to the funding."

"Then what's in the safe deposit box?" Aidan asked. "And is that what the thieves were looking for on Wednesday night?"

"The only way we're going to know that is to fly up there on Monday and open it ourselves."

Chapter 16

Wrestling Match

Aidan

Saturday morning over breakfast, Aidan turned to Edwin. "The rabbi asked if we could provide something for him to say about Darius. Would you like to write something?"

Edwin shook his head. "I am still struggling to make sense of everything I've learned since he died."

"Would you like me to, based on what you have told me?"

"That would be lovely. And he had a diary you could read if you want more. It's on the shelf in his office." He smiled. "Many years ago, a company published a blank book they called *The Nothing Book*. Darius's father had died and he was trying to remember everything about his childhood. So I bought him a copy of that book and told him to start writing."

"Have you read it?" Aidan asked.

Edwin shook his head. "Back then, he said the memories were too raw and he wasn't ready to share them. I don't even know if he kept it up."

After they finished eating, Aidan went up to the office

to look for the diary, and found it on a shelf. The paper jacket showed evidence of regular reading, with tiny tears along the edges. He sat behind Darius's desk and opened it to the first page.

Darius had beautiful penmanship, probably the result of all his drafting lessons, and quickly Aidan was drawn in.

"I was born in Shiraz, a lovely city of gardens and poets. My father was a musician, so our home was full of beauty and music. He could play any stringed instrument, including several in the family of long-necked lutes, and he had a deep baritone voice. But musicians were not paid well, and sometimes he ran up against the mullahs who disapproved of some of his repertoire."

Darius had drawn beautiful renderings of several of the instruments on the following pages, and even attempted a rough sketch of his father, bent over one of those long-necked lutes. It was captioned "Bāba with tar."

Aidan felt the emotion rising from the page. Here was a man who loved his father.

He kept turning the pages. "We always had plenty to eat, with lamb or beef stew over rice, lavash bread, and sheep's milk cheese. My mother's rice pudding flavored with rose water was my favorite dessert."

Here Darius had sketched a glass bowl filled with a creamy white pudding, decorated with red rose petals. Aidan's mouth watered. There were also drawings of fruits and vegetables, each rendered with the same care and attention to detail. They were almost museum-quality, and Aidan wondered if Darius had ever polished any of them for framing. But he hadn't noticed anything like those sketches on the walls of the house, only photographs of Darius's designer garments.

Liam came into the office. "What are you reading?"

"Darius's diary. He had so much talent." He held up the page he was looking at. "Aren't these beautiful drawings?"

Liam looked closely. "Beautiful enough to make me hungry," he said. "You've been up here for a couple of hours. Coming down for lunch?"

Aidan pulled out the red fabric bookmark and left it where he stopped reading, and went downstairs. He put together a sandwich platter and the three of them ate at the kitchen table. "You really should look at Darius's diary," Aidan said. "I've been reading it, and it's giving me a real sense of who he is. Or at least, who he was back then."

"He was a dreamer," Edwin said. "Full of plans and ideas. Sometimes we'd be at a restaurant and he'd see a woman pass by, and he'd grab a napkin and start sketching. Some of his most beautiful creations came that way."

He waved his hand around the room. "You only have to look around to see how he wanted to surround himself with beauty. I was the drabbest thing in his life."

"You aren't drab at all," Aidan said. "Look at what you're wearing. That shirt is a riot of colors, and your slacks are perfectly tailored. You make a good impression."

"It's all Darius's doing," Edwin said. "I knew nothing about fashion when I met him. Sure, I knew about the business side, but I had no sense of my own style. What you see in front of you is all Darius's creation."

After lunch, Edwin returned to his room, and Liam said, "I'm feeling rusty with all this sitting around eating good food. We need to exercise to stay on our game. We still have no idea what we're up against."

They moved some furniture around in the living room to clear a space to work out. They wore tank tops and shorts, all made from material that wicked away sweat. They began with stretching, and Aidan felt his muscles begin to loosen as he shook out his shoulders, bent his arms and legs, and swiveled his neck around.

They had a regular yoga routine, beginning with *Savasana*, their legs straight as they focused on breathing. Reclining twists, then the cat and cow positions, abdominal crunches and the *balasana*, or child's pose. They finished with downward facing dog, then pivoted into the warrior asana, with knees bent and arms outstretched.

"We've been lazy," Liam said. "I can feel it in my muscles. As we get older we have to work harder."

"Or not," Aidan said. "We can take on less dangerous jobs. Focus on strategy instead of brute strength."

Liam looked at him like he was speaking a foreign language. "Come on, Liam, you know that we can't do this kind of work forever. We have to come up with an exit strategy at some point."

"We tried that, with Louis and Hassan," Liam said. "Corporate security consulting, remember? And that was a bust."

"That's not the only path we can take," Aidan said. "We could both teach, for example. Set up our own courses in close protection."

"That's a huge operation," Liam protested. "Remember that class you took in Georgia, when you first decided to work with me? They had a shooting range and a driving course. How many instructors did they have?"

"Five," Aidan said. "But that was an introductory course so they had to cover a lot of material. Sixty hours of classwork and I got a certification at the end. We could do advanced training based on what we've learned. How working with Arabs is different from other groups. And we've had a lot more experience investigating threats than most close protection specialists ever get."

"It's something to think about," Liam said. "Now let's continue."

He assumed the starting wrestling stance, with his feet shoulder-width apart, his weight evenly distributed, and his knees slightly bent.

Aidan mimicked his position, then held back and waited for his husband to make the first move. Liam was taller and stronger, so it was better to make him the aggressor, and for Aidan to use his wits and his own strength to fight back.

It was what they needed to do in protecting clients as well, Aidan thought. Assume a defensive stance and wait for an attack. But there had already been three attacks—Darius's death, the attempted break-in before they arrived, and the second on Wednesday night. How long would they sit around waiting for something else?

They head-locked, then Aidan managed to kick Liam's leg out from under him and they fell to the carpet. Then the wrestling match was really on, in a way they hadn't struggled in a long time. They grunted and sweated and pulled at each other's clothing.

Aidan had just yanked Liam's shorts down, exposing his well-filled jockstrap, when they heard a cough. They both stopped, sweaty despite the air conditioning, and looked up. "Sorry to interrupt you," Edwin said. "But I got a phone call."

Chapter 17

A Beautiful Place

Aidan

They separated, and Liam quickly pulled his shorts back up. "Who called you?" Aidan asked.

"Harvey Grant. He asked if I'd had a chance to find Darius's will yet. And if I have access to his bank accounts."

Aidan grabbed a towel and dried his face. "What did you tell him?"

"I played the grieving widower. Haven't had a chance to look at anything. I said that I have access to all our joint accounts so I can pay the bills, and I'll wait to settle anything else until I feel better."

"Good move," Liam stood up. "I think I'll go for a swim. Either of you want to join me?"

"I'm going to shower and go back to Darius's journal," Aidan said.

"I'll pass on swimming," Edwin said. "That was always Darius's thing. I prefer pickleball."

Aidan smiled. "You don't mind if Liam swims in the nude, do you?" he asked.

Liam was not amused. "Aidan."

"The pool is very sheltered," Edwin said. "The only place you can see it is from Darius's office. So you don't have to worry about anyone checking you out." He smiled. "Even a blood relative."

Liam blushed, which Aidan thought was adorable. But his husband was an exhibitionist, and used to shower nude in the courtyard of the house behind the Bar Mamounia, his assets on display to everyone.

After he showered and dressed, Aidan sat back down at Darius's desk with his journal, looking for insights into the man, and things he might mention in his eulogy the next day.

"Isfahan was a beautiful place of gardens and colorful mosques with elaborately patterned domes," he read. "Women in chadors walked with others in modern dress. The cinema brought European culture to us at the same time that women washed and dried carpets in Shahr-e Ray the way they had done for centuries."

This was accompanied by sketches of gardens draped in hanging vines, beautiful mosques, and one large drawing of carpets laid out to dry along a hilly slope. Darius's attention to detail was amazing—each of the carpets had an intricate pattern, and the shading of each one was realistic.

Aidan continued reading. "We didn't have a lot of money for clothes," Darius wrote. "Fortunately my father's mother was an expert at needlework, and she made everything we wore. I spent many hours at her side, learning how to measure, cut and stitch fabric. From an early age I began to design my own clothes, flowing shirts with pointed collars and open necks and loose-legged pants that were nothing like the drab shirts and short pants the other boys wore. They teased me and threw stones at me, and whenever it rained they delighted in splashing mud on me."

Aidan sat back. He hated to read anything about bullying. He had been lucky as a boy and a teen. He wasn't overtly effeminate, and he had his own friends, mostly other outcasts. Though he had been called names, he had a wicked tongue himself, and he threw back sharp insults at anyone who dared him. For the most part, the bullies left him alone.

Darius had drawn in some sketches of himself as a boy and what he was wearing. His face was usually turned away or looking down. The focus was always on the clothes.

"My grandmother is the one who inspired me to study fashion, and she died as I was about to begin my course in Tehran. My first year, my hands were slippery with tears as I tried to remember all her lessons."

Here Darius had drawn several sketches of his grandmother, her face all sharp angles, her fingers gnarled as she clutched a pair of scissors or a sewing needle. Places on the page had been spattered with liquid, probably Darius's tears. They moved him.

Darius wrote about the fashion institute instructors who inspired him, and his discoveries of the properties of fabrics his grandmother had never touched, silk, satin, and fibers woven from the hair of animals only seen in the zoological garden in Isfahan.

The next pages were filled with drawings he had created for his classwork, elegant gowns for willowy women. Sometimes Aidan could see Darius sketching his own face onto those women.

The diary petered out after that, as if Darius had said all he wanted to about his life. Aidan turned to the computer and began to compose some words he or Edwin might read at the funeral.

As they sat down to dinner, he showed what he had

written to Edwin. "I wrote this up based on what you've said about Darius, and what I read in his journal. Would you like to add anything?"

He handed a piece of paper to Edwin, who read it and then began to cry. "It's lovely," he said. "How could you capture him so well without ever knowing him?"

"I've been listening to you. Do you think you'll want to say something yourself?"

Edwin shook his head. "I know I'll fall apart, and Darius would hate that."

Aidan threw together a pasta dish with whatever was left from his shopping expedition. "Do you want the rabbi to invite people to come over here tomorrow after the funeral?" Aidan asked. "Even if you don't want to do the whole sitting shiva thing, it's a Jewish tradition, and it gives people a chance to express their emotions."

"Do you think it's safe?" Edwin asked. "What if whoever tried to break in comes to the funeral and then follows us here?"

Aidan looked at Liam, who shrugged. "We'll watch over you," Aidan said. "And maybe this is a chance to draw someone out. Give us a better clue as to what we're dealing with."

"If you want," Edwin said.

Liam followed Aidan into the kitchen. "Should we have someone stay here while we're at the cemetery?" Aidan asked.

"Who would we ask? We need both of us to watch Edwin."

"We could call Detective Tseng and ask her to station a car outside while we're gone."

"Call her on a Saturday evening?" Liam asked. "She already thinks Edwin is overreacting."

"I suppose. But it worries me. I keep remembering my great-aunt's friend. How my family worried about someone breaking in during a funeral."

"We can't put a friend of Edwin's at risk," Liam said. "We'll have to play it as it goes."

They returned to the dining room. "Our next step in figuring out what happened to Darius is to know what's in that safe deposit box in Washington," Liam said. "Are you up to traveling there with us?"

"I'm not staying here without you," Edwin said. "And I want to know what Darius was involved in." He turned to Aidan. "Can you make the arrangements?"

"I'll do it after dinner. Anywhere special you want to stay?"

"I'll reserve a suite at the Washington Diplomat, the hotel where Darius and I usually stayed," Edwin said. "Certainly not the Holiday Inn Express. I'm surprised that Darius didn't complain that the sheets there made him itch. Though that was probably another secret he kept from me."

After dinner Aidan made reservations for them on a Monday morning flight to Reagan National. As he finished, he looked up to see Edwin in the doorway. "What's up?"

"He was dying," he said, and burst into tears once more.

Chapter 18

Thoughts of Home
Aidan

"You're talking about Darius?" Aidan asked, as Liam joined them.

Edwin nodded and handed Aidan a manila folder full of test results and doctors' notes. "I'll save you the trouble of reading it all," Edwin said. "He had stage three multiple myeloma."

Liam walked over and took Edwin by the arm, and led him to a chair at the table. "Did you know that?" he asked.

Edwin wiped his eyes on his sleeve. "I knew he wasn't feeling his best, and that the doctors were running tests. I didn't realize he had been diagnosed, or that it was so serious."

"Did they give him a timetable?" Aidan asked.

"According to what's here, the five-year survival rate is thirty-five percent. But depending on the patient, he could have had only a few months or a year left."

Aidan had an idea. "Did he ever talk about going back to Iran?"

Edwin nodded. "He wanted to go back to Isfahan, where he grew up, and visit his parents' graves. But he was worried about the regime's approach to homosexuality. He thought that they knew he was gay because they monitor the US media, and because our marriage license is public record. He was afraid that if he went back there they'd arrest him."

"I've read about US citizens of Iranian descent who are arrested and kept in prison," Liam said. "I'd certainly never encourage a gay client, or one with a political profile that was opposed to the regime, to travel there."

"Darius knew that. I think maybe that's why he was willing to listen to Harvey Grant and put money behind this organization. That if they could topple the mullahs he could go home again."

They sat together for a while longer, talking about Darius's motivations, and how they might have led to his death. Eventually Edwin went to sleep, and Aidan and Liam went up to their room.

"Let's talk about the funeral tomorrow," Liam said. "I pulled up a street view of the cemetery this afternoon and it looks defensible. A flat piece of land with visibility to all four corners. They don't have upright headstones where someone could hide—all the markers are the flat kind."

"What about the street?" Aidan asked. "Could someone park at the street and have an angle toward Edwin?"

Liam shook his head. "Two-lane road, so nowhere to stop. We won't know exactly where the grave is until we get to the cemetery, but I'll keep an eye out as people pull up and park in case anyone lingers by the cars."

"When I made the arrangements, the counselor told me there would be a canopy over the grave with chairs underneath. So the only way someone can get a clear shot is going to and from the grave."

Liam nodded. "That's good to know. Even though

Edwin is my cousin, you're better at the emotional stuff, so I'd like you to stick by him, and I'll stay back and stand lookout." He frowned. "I wish we knew how many people to expect."

"No way to know. Edwin and Darius were both very connected in this community. I think we'll get people Edwin knew through his charity work, neighbors. Maybe other Iranians that Darius knew."

"Those will be the people to watch out for."

Aidan yawned. "I'm sorry Darius won't have family there to say goodbye to him. When my father passed away, his brother was alive, and my aunt and uncle were there, along with my cousin Ellen and her husband. And we still had lots of cousins in Trenton to come to my mother's funeral."

"That must have been tough for you, being an only child. You had Blake then, didn't you?"

"I hadn't met him by the time my father died, but my mother had a chance to meet him a few times. He didn't come to her funeral, though."

"Really?"

Aidan crossed his arms over his chest. "He wasn't comfortable with death. His parents were still alive, and his grandparents. I don't think he'd ever been to a funeral in his life. To him it was just another social engagement, one he could get out of because he had to work."

"What a jerk."

"I tried to tell him that funerals aren't for the dead, they're for the living. To comfort the ones left behind. He took me out to dinner that night, but I wasn't good company, and he used that as a reason why he hadn't come to the cemetery. Because he knew I would be moody."

"I wish I could have been there for you."

"You're here now, and that's what matters," Aidan said. "I don't know how I'd feel if we weren't allowed to come back to the States," he said. "To never see the place where I grew up again, to be forbidden from seeing my parents' graves."

"I don't have the same connection to home that you do," Liam said, pulling his polo shirt over his head. Aidan took a moment to marvel at his husband's muscles, then looked away.

"I know," he said. "But you must have some good memories of growing up."

"I do." Liam dropped his shorts and then wiggled out of his jockstrap. He stretched, his ample penis at parade rest. "Mostly of being small and having treats, like going to Dairy Queen or having a field day at school." He slipped into bed as Aidan pulled off his own shorts, but kept his boxers on.

Liam leaned back against the pillows, his hands behind his head. "Doris had a friend who lived in Highland Park, right across the Raritan River from where we lived, and sometimes she'd take the three of us there to meet her friend and the friend's kids. We went to a candy store there that had a soda fountain, and each of us got to pick one flavor of ice cream for a sundae."

He smiled. "I always got peppermint stick. They had the greatest hot fudge sauce. It was a family-owned place, and when one of the daughters, Becky, was making the sundaes she always added extra hot fudge for us."

He turned on his side as Aidan slid into bed beside him. "I remember Frannie pocketed an ashtray from the ice cream company, Moglia's. My mom used to stub out her Lucky Strikes. I'm surprised that none of us has lung cancer considering how much she smoked."

"It's nice that you have a few good memories," Aidan said.

"I'm sure that candy store is closed now. Probably replaced by a bubble tea place."

Aidan snuggled in beside him, and Liam leaned down and kissed the top of his head. "Making better memories with you," he said.

Aidan looked up with a smile. "Do any of them involve hot fudge?"

"Only on ice cream, sweetheart," Liam said. "Only on ice cream."

Aidan turned on his side as Liam fell asleep. It was so warm and comforting to have his husband beside him. He felt a moment of sadness for Edwin, who had given up this kind of physical connection with Darius years before. It was up to him and Liam to see that Edwin was safe and could have the chance to find some solace again.

Chapter 19

The Beauty of the Lord
Aidan

Sunday morning Aidan drove to Whole Foods again, and picked up a couple of platters of food to put out for guests. He and Edwin spent some time in the living room, removing items from tabletops so guests would have a place to put a glass or a plate down.

It was a gorgeous day, the sky a pale blue dotted with a few white clouds. The temperature was in the low seventies and there was a light breeze. At ten-thirty, they dressed in somber clothing and drove to the cemetery, where they found a canopy beside an open grave, with four chairs underneath it, protected from the sun. Aidan saw the pile of dirt beside the open grave.

"Have you ever been to a Jewish funeral before?" he asked Edwin.

Edwin shook his head.

"Things will be very simple," Aidan said. "The rabbi will welcome the mourners and probably say a few words about death. Then a few prayers. I'll give him what I wrote about Darius so that he can either read it or extrapolate from it as a eulogy. Then a few more prayers, and then we'll each step up and put a shovel full of dirt onto the coffin."

Edwin looked horrified. "Really? Don't they have people to do that?"

"It's a Jewish tradition," Aidan said. "To symbolize that the deceased has returned to where he came from – man comes from the earth, and so must he return to earth. And the survivors are here to help with that journey."

"Sounds barbaric to me," Edwin said. "But I want Darius to have the funeral he would have wanted."

As they turned into the driveway that led to the office, Aidan checked the rear-view mirror. No one was following them, which was good. However, the last time he'd been to a cemetery with Liam, in north Jersey, they'd had a squad of government agents to protect them, and things had gotten ugly.

They parked beside the office, which was a short distance from the canopy. When Edwin got out, he said, "The sky is the color of Tiffany boxes. That was Darius's favorite jewelry brand. He loved their cufflinks, and I bought him a different pair for every birthday." He stifled a sob, and Aidan put his arm around his shoulders.

Liam let them walk a few feet ahead and trailed behind, looking right and left. He held the door open and then followed them inside.

Aidan introduced them to the receptionist, and a few moments later the rabbi came out of an office at the rear. He was a young man in a dark suit and hand-crocheted blue-and-white yarmulke. "I'm Rabbi Golan." He looked to the three of them.

Edwin held out his hand. "Edwin McCullough. Darius was my husband. And this is my cousin Liam, and his husband Aidan."

The Designer of His Own Fortune

Rabbi Golan shook hands with each of them, then Aidan handed him what he had written. "Some details about Darius's life you might want to use in talking about him," he said. "Edwin would prefer not to speak himself."

The rabbi scanned through it. "This is excellent," he said.

Aidan handed him one more piece of paper. "I found this in Darius's journal," he said. "It looks like a Persian version of the 27th Psalm. It might be nice if you could read this. Particularly the fourth verse."

The rabbi read out, "One thing I ask of the LORD, this is what I seek: that I may dwell in the house of the LORD all the days of my life, to gaze upon the beauty of the LORD and to seek him in his temple." He looked up from the paper. "It's lovely. And Mr. Ashoori sounds like someone who lived his life in pursuit of beauty."

"That he did," Edwin turned to Aidan. "I'm so pleased you found that."

Aidan squeezed Edwin's hand as the rabbi went through a few more details of the graveside service. Aidan gave him the address on Gentle Rain Drive, where Edwin would be sitting shiva that afternoon.

Liam led the way outside, scanning the area. An elderly woman sat on a stool beside a grave, as if she was talking to the occupant. Across the way, a middle-aged couple laid pebbles on top of a gravestone, a reminder that the person buried there had been loved and visited by someone who mourned them.

The three of them followed the rabbi out of the cemetery office to the grave. As they neared it, Edwin's steps faltered. "I don't think I can do this."

This time it was Liam who took his arm. "You can," he said. "For Darius."

"For Darius," Edwin repeatedly softly.

Liam stood point at the edge of the street as cars began to arrive and mourners stepped out. Most of them were around Edwin's age, and appeared to be people he knew from his charitable works. He spoke to each one, shaking hands and thanking them for coming.

Aidan assessed each one as he or she stepped up. Despite the clues that led them to someone involved with Iran, he couldn't discount the possibility that Darius had been killed by, or on the orders of, someone in Boca. He listened closely to each conversation, but no one asked about Darius's will or the circumstances of his death.

Edwin called Liam over to meet one woman in her sixties. "This is my cousin Mary Elizabeth," he said. "On the Gallagher side." He turned to the woman. "My cousin Liam McCullough. Aunt Doris's son."

She shook Liam's hand. "I've heard about you. I only met your mother once but it was a memorable experience."

"I'm sure," Liam said.

"And this is his husband, Aidan," Edwin said. "Mary Elizabeth splits her time between a house in Short Hills and a condo here in Boca."

"It's very kind of you to come," Aidan said to the woman.

"It's a terrible thing. But family needs to stick together."

Liam returned to his guard duty, and Aidan escorted Edwin to the front row of seats. Aidan sat to one side of him, Mary Elizabeth on the other. Other chairs were taken by people who needed them. Liam stood to the side of the group, alert to anything that was going on around them.

A handsome young man, probably in his mid to late twenties, arrived as the rabbi was about to being speaking, and he stood to the side of the mourners. Aidan noticed that Liam kept an eye on him, watching for unexpected movement.

The rabbi recited a few blessings, then read what Aidan had written. "It's clear that Mr. Ashoori was a valued member of his community," the rabbi said when he finished. "Would anyone else like to say a few words?"

He looked to Edwin, who shook his head. Then the young man Aidan had spotted earlier stepped up. He had black hair and heavy eyebrows, with the kind of two-day beard that was common among young men. His face was square, his jaw strong, and Aidan wondered if he had ever modeled for Darius—in or out of clothing. He wore a blue satin yarmulke, probably from someone's wedding or bar mitzvah.

"I didn't know Mr. Ashoori well, but he was very kind to me. I'm studying for my PhD in Middle Eastern history at the University of Miami, and many of my source materials are in Farsi."

Aidan leaned close to Edwin. "That must be Parviz Esfahani. Darius emailed him regularly."

Edwin stared at the man as he continued. "Mr. Ashoori helped me understand them—not just what was written, but how the actions written about in those documents affected real people. We met regularly for coffee and those lessons. Even the afternoon of his death, we talked at a Starbucks near the Town Center before he did his shopping."

Then he stepped aside. The rabbi mentioned that Edwin would be receiving visitors at the home on Gentle Rain Drive, and then picked up a shovel that had been stuck in the pile of dirt. "A Jewish tradition is for each mourner to place three shovelfuls of dirt into the grave," he said. "For the first, the shovel is held so that the back of the shovel faces upward, to show that it is being used for a purpose that's the opposite of life. Using the shovel that way takes extra time, showing our reluctance to bury a loved one."

He held the shovel upward for the first pass, then in the regular position for the next two. Then he stuck the shovel back into the dirt and looked at the mourners.

Edwin rose, with Aidan at his arm, and he cried as he mimicked the rabbi's actions. Then he stepped back and Aidan performed the ritual. Many of the mourners followed, except Liam, who remained at the edge of the street, watching everything.

A cool breeze swept across the cemetery, moving a few dead leaves ahead of it. The rabbi spoke as the last person was putting dirt on the grave. "Would all the mourners please form two lines for the family to exit," he said.

Edwin shook his hand. "No, no, I don't want any fuss. Everyone can leave. And if anyone wants to drop by the house, they're welcome."

As the mourners began to walk toward their cars, Aidan left Edwin to Liam and made a beeline for the young man. "Excuse me, are you Parviz Esfahani?"

"I am."

"I'm Aidan Greene, and my husband is Edwin's cousin. We'd love to talk to you about your connection with Darius. Could I get your phone number?"

"Certainly. But I'm leaving tomorrow morning for a research trip to the Middle East, and I'll be out of touch for at least a week."

"Do you have a few minutes now?" Aidan asked. "You could come to the house."

"I could. I've never been there, but I have the address in my phone."

The Designer of His Own Fortune

Suddenly Edwin's phone began to shriek with an unusual tone. He fumbled it from his pocket. "It's the alarm," he said. "Someone's breaking into the house. Again."

He looked at Liam and Aidan. "Will it ever stop?"

Chapter 20

Parviz

Liam

"The police will get there before we can," Liam said. "But I'm going to call Detective Tseng."

Edwin shut down the signal on his phone and Aidan hustled him back to the SUV. Liam called Tseng's cell and let her know about the break-in.

"I'm on my way," she said.

By the time they reached Boca Largo, a police cruiser was parked on Gentle Rain Drive in front of the house, the overhead lights flashing. Aidan pulled into the driveway and Liam jumped out.

The front door had been pried open, and one of the officers stood there. Liam identified himself to the man, whose tag read Sanchez. "My partner is around the back," Sanchez said. "We haven't gone into the house yet, but the thieves probably ran off as soon as they heard the alarm."

Sanchez's partner, a rail-thin woman named Porowski, came around the side of the house. "Rear is clear. But I saw through the back window they did a quick ransack of the living room."

Edwin and Aidan approached, and Edwin said, "You

knew this was going to happen. Why didn't you do anything to prevent it?"

"We didn't know," Aidan said.

"You talked about it last night in the kitchen. I heard you. Something about a man named Sid Levy who was hired to guard houses while people were at funerals."

"It was a woman," Aidan said. "A friend of my great-aunt's. And I never heard of anyone breaking into a house like that. It was an old folk tale."

"One that came true in Boca Raton." Edwin turned to Officer Porowski. "How bad is it?"

"I didn't get a close look," she said. "Sofa cushions tossed around, drawers dumped open."

"Can we go inside?" Edwin asked.

"I'll go in first." Liam was worried that the thief might have discovered their small cache of weapons and taken them, leaving him and Aidan defenseless.

He prowled around the living room, which was as Officer Porowski had said. "Downstairs is clear," he called back to those outside.

He climbed the stairs silently, on the off-chance that someone was still up there. But as he moved from room to room, he found nothing. There must have been at least two men, because someone had been into Darius's office, and it was unlikely one man would have had enough time to search both floors before fleeing the klaxon blare of the alarm.

When Liam returned downstairs, Detective Tseng had arrived. She called for a crime scene team and asked the two officers to wait outside.

Then she, Aidan, and Edwin joined Liam for a full walk-through. "Can you tell if anything was taken?" Tseng asked Edwin.

Edwin shook his head. "We had already cleared these surfaces, stowing away any breakables to prepare for visitors after the funeral."

"It's clear whoever was here was looking for something," Tseng said. "You have any idea what?"

Aidan looked at Liam. Should they tell Tseng about the key to the safe deposit box?

"Paperwork?" Tseng asked. "You looked at Mr. Ashoori's will, didn't you? Did it have anything relevant?"

Edwin shook his head. "Nothing we didn't know about. And Darius's business was sold years ago. Everything related to that has long since been digitized."

"Well, I suggest you think that through."

A car pulled up along the street, and Edwin looked outside. "Oh, Lord. People are arriving."

"You don't want to bring strangers into the house until we've dusted for prints," Tseng said.

"What if we take them around to the patio?" Aidan asked. "It's cool enough. I can bring the platters out there, and you can talk while the police finish their business."

"That sounds like a good idea," Tseng said.

Edwin went out front to greet the mourners who had arrived, and Aidan and Liam began ferrying food and drinks out to the back patio. They kept busy filling glasses and providing plates and napkins as about a dozen people, some of them neighbors, arrived.

When Liam spotted Parviz Esfahani he spoke to Aidan, and the two of them walked around to the front of the house.

"What's going on?" Parviz asked.

"Someone broke into the house while we were at the cemetery," Aidan said.

"Really? That's terrible. I knew Mr. Ashoori was

wealthy but I assumed he had the right security measures in place. Some of his political positions might have put him in danger."

"That's what we wanted to talk to you about," Liam said.

Tseng came to the front door of the house. "The crime scene team are finished. You'll want to clean up some of the fingerprint powder."

"I can manage that," Aidan said. "Liam, why don't you and Parviz find a corner of the living room where you can talk. I'll tell Edwin what we're doing."

The police all left, and Liam led Parviz into the living room. He picked up some loose sofa cushions and made a corner where he and the young man could sit.

Aidan came into the living room with a spray bottle and kitchen rags and began cleaning.

"You mentioned Darius's political positions," Liam said. "Can you say anything more about that?"

Parviz nodded. "When I met Darius, he was very much a monarchist. He was close to the Shahbanu and her son, and he believed the best thing for Persia was to put a Pahlavi back on the Peacock Throne."

"That's what we understood from his husband," Liam said.

"But he began to change his mind during the winter," Parviz said. "He asked me all kinds of questions about things the old shah did during his reign, and some unsavory practices the monarchist groups were engaging in."

"Such as?"

"Repression, torture, refusal to be open to alternative points of view."

"Did he have evidence of any of this?" Liam asked, as Aidan paused in his cleaning to listen in.

"He said that he'd seen documents," Parviz said. "Videos and testimonies." He shuddered. "He described some of them to me. Terrible things."

"And that evidence changed his mind?"

Parviz nodded. "Gradually, as I said."

He hesitated. "He told me that he had received some bad health news, and that he wanted to return to Persia before he died, but couldn't see doing that with the mullahs in charge. By March, he had shifted his support to one of the democratic groups. A small one, but one with a lot of support in Iran. Many people who were willing to take risks to spy on the mullahs and report their doings. He felt they were the best hope to bring down the current regime."

"But not to reinstall the shah's son."

"No. He told me he saw a new draft of the constitution for Iran. It called for a democracy based on ideas and ideologies, rather than on religions and tribal identities."

"Is that realistic?" Liam asked. "My understanding of the Middle East is that it has long been dominated by tribal factions."

"Iran is different. Over two-thirds of Iran's population are ethnic Persians, which unites them. There are smaller groups of Azeris, Kurds, and Turkish people, but as long as they are treated fairly they will go along with the majority."

Aidan gave up on cleaning and sat with them. "Was Darius worried about anyone? The current government? Perhaps a monarchist group that resented his defection?"

"He told me he had to be very careful. He used a very secure email service when communicating with this group, and any money he donated to them went to an untraceable account. I had to vet anything I wrote about him on my blog."

"How big is your audience?" Aidan asked.

"I have about five thousand followers. For the most part I blog about history, but occasionally I write about politics as well. I have heard from many people in the US government and abroad who appreciate what I write."

Edwin joined them in the living room. "This is a mess," he said. "I'm glad we didn't invite everyone inside."

Parviz rose. "My deepest sympathies, Mr. Gallagher. Mr. Ashoori was a very special man and I was privileged to know him."

"And did you fuck him?" Edwin said brightly.

Parviz's mouth dropped open. "Our relationship was nothing like that. He was an honorable man and he was devoted to you." He turned to Aidan and Liam. "And now, I must leave to get ready for my trip."

Chapter 21

Calling Louis

Aidan

Edwin sunk down into a sofa. "I don't know what came over me. I'm so embarrassed."

"We were learning some useful information," Liam said. "I doubt we'll get any more out of Mr. Esfahani now."

Edwin began to sob. "I know, I'm stupid. That was unforgivable."

Aidan sat beside him and put his arm around Edwin's shoulders. "He's a handsome man, and Darius was wealthy and charming. It was a reasonable guess, even if it wasn't true."

"I want something to make sense of Darius's death," Edwin said. "To make the pain of losing him less."

"Sometimes the only way to deal with pain is to live through it," Aidan said. "When my ex dumped me, I went a little crazy. Flew halfway around the world to get away from him, for a job that never materialized."

"How did you manage?"

"I met a sexy bodyguard who needed my help for a trip through the Sahara. Fell in love, got shot at by bad guys.

Ended up in the middle of a battle between terrorists and the US Navy."

Edwin stopped crying and stared at him. "I hope you're not suggesting that for me. My passport is expired."

Aidan stared back at him, until the edges of Edwin's eyes crinkled with a smile, and they both laughed. "Yeah, it's not the best solution for everyone. But the idea is the same. Do something different instead of sitting around feeling bad."

"Fortunately I don't need a passport to go to Washington," Edwin said. "I am really eager to see what Darius stashed away in that safe deposit box."

They called Anthony Colasanto, the same locksmith who had opened the safe, and he came over to strip out the damaged lock on the front door and replace it with a new, better one. He put the same lock on the rear door as well.

"You'll feel safe with these locks," Colasanto said. "It's the next generation of lock security. Solid, hardened steel casing and inserts make it drill-proof and impervious to attacks from crowbars and other common tools."

"Sounds good to me," Edwin said.

After Colasanto left, the three of them worked together to clean up the house. "You don't think whoever broke in will keep trying, do you?" Edwin asked as they plumped the last pillows.

"I can't speculate on what they'll do," Liam said. "We don't have enough information."

"That's not very helpful, Liam." Aidan turned to Edwin. "The new locks are going to make it harder to break in, and Liam and I will be here with you tonight."

"But what about the future?" Edwin asked. "You're not going to stay here with me for the rest of my life."

"Tomorrow we fly to DC and see what's in the safe

deposit box. And then we figure out how to get rid of it so that no one has a reason to come after you." Aidan looked at Liam, who nodded.

Edwin was on edge through dinner, as Aidan expected him to be. Liam took Edwin with him as he walked around the house before bed, showing him that each door and window was secured before engaging the alarm system. Then Liam joined Aidan in what had been Darius's bedroom.

"This is a mess." Liam stalked over to the window that looked out over the back yard.

"I agree," Aidan said, from his place on the bed. "But we might be able to find some answers in that safe deposit box tomorrow."

Liam turned back to him. "But what if we don't? How long are we going to hang around here while stuff keeps happening?"

"You know the answer to that, Liam. We're going to stay with Edwin until we find out where the threat is coming from and neutralize it."

Liam crossed his arms over his chest and stared. "We should never have taken this job."

"Because he's your cousin? Because he's forcing you to confront things about your family?"

Liam curled his lip. "Sometimes you are too perceptive."

"That's what fifteen years together does for you," Aidan said. "I can read you like a book. Like a book in Braille that I can run my fingers over." He smiled and flexed his fingers at his husband, who smiled.

"I could do with some of those fingers," Liam said.

He pulled his polo shirt over his head, and Aidan

marveled at all the musculature. "You want a back rub?" he asked.

"Would I ever turn one down?"

"Darius left some massage oil in the dresser drawer," Aidan said. "Want to get that?"

"You don't know what he was using that for."

Aidan laughed. "Don't be a prude. So he greased his dick with it. Big deal. Maybe if you're lucky I'll do the same for you later."

"I've been lucky since I met you," Liam said.

Monday morning Aidan served up a breakfast of orange juice and muffins, and they left Boca early and drove to the Fort Lauderdale airport in the rental car. Aidan noticed Liam checking regularly to make sure they weren't being followed. He dropped Edwin and Liam at the terminal and returned the car, and then met them at the gate.

The airport had a festive air, even though it was mid-October. Florida was a vacation destination, and there were groups all around. Black women in matching sorority T-shirts, families with piles of luggage, and couples holding onto the tropical mood in patterned shirts and shorts. Steel drum music played through the speakers.

Each of them had a small carry-on bag with a change of clothes. Even if they resolved Edwin's problems, Aidan would only feel comfortable returning him to Boca safely. They had to leave behind the expanding batons and the switchblade knives, and that worried him. With each step forward, they were leaving something behind that they might need.

Because they were in business class, they boarded early,

with Edwin in a window seat and Liam beside him, and Aidan on the other side of the aisle. Liam was alert until they closed the airplane doors, then he slept all the way to Washington.

Aidan envied him. He kept thinking about Darius's death and the three break-ins at the house. It was frustrating that they couldn't figure out where the threat was coming from. It didn't make sense that someone would kill Darius, then try to steal something he had left behind. Why not force Darius to give up whatever it was, on threat of death?

They landed easily, and the three of them were among the first people off the plane. Reagan National was bustling with tourists, businesspeople, and government wonks. This was a serious airport, less frivolous than Fort Lauderdale. They traversed the long hallway between the gates, with its tall windows facing on the runway, and followed the signs to the taxi rank.

Aidan gave the driver the address of the bank, and when they walked in Edwin asked for a manager to show him to the box. It had been registered only in Darius's name, so Edwin brought a copy of their marriage certificate, Edwin's will, and the death certificate they'd gotten at the funeral home.

The branch manager showed them to a small room and used the key they'd found in the safe, along with his own key, to open the box. Then he left them there.

"No time like the present," Edwin said, and popped the lid of the box. Inside was a manila folder stuffed with paperwork, as well as a one-terabyte jump drive. With Liam and Aidan looking over his shoulder, Edwin opened the folder.

Many of the pages were government documents marked confidential. There were photographs and copies of passport pages. Lots of lists of names and places, some in

English, some in Farsi. "We probably shouldn't even be looking at this," Liam said.

"Where the hell did Darius get this material?" Edwin asked.

"Harvey Grant?" Aidan and Liam spoke in tandem, and unthinkingly, both of them said "Jinx" at the same time.

"Then we should return these pages to him," Edwin said. "I don't want to be responsible for them."

"What if they didn't come from Grant, though?" Liam asked. "We already know that he has lied to us. Perhaps it's Grant who has sent someone to find these documents."

"This is all beyond me," Edwin said.

Aidan looked at Liam. "You're the one with government experience. What do you suggest we do?"

"I suggest we call Louis and see what he thinks."

Chapter 22

Room Service

Liam

"Just the right time to disrupt his dinner." Liam turned to his cousin. "Louis Fleck is a close friend who used to work for the CIA and the State Department, and he still has a lot of contacts there."

He pulled out his cell phone. "No bars here. This room is probably shielded. I don't think we have much choice. We're going to have to take this material with us so that I can describe it accurately when we get hold of Louis."

Aidan put the folder and the jump drive in his backpack, and Liam closed the drawer and slid it back into place. Then they left the room, thanking the manager on their way out.

Another cab, this one to the Washington Diplomat Hotel, a boutique property on Capitol Hill. The manager came to the front desk as Edwin prepared to check in. "Welcome back, Mr. Gallagher," he said. "Will Mr. Ashoori be joining you as well?"

"Darius passed away last week," Edwin said.

"I'm so sorry for your loss. We have your regular suite prepared for you, if you'd like."

"Yes, that would be fine. We can take our own luggage, though."

Edwin led the way to the elevator, and then to the suite, which was the epitome of simple luxury. The curtain swags and upholstery were elegant enough for Darius, yet the white furniture and beige carpeting plain enough for Edwin. He took his bag into his room, leaving Aidan and Liam in the living room.

"Why don't you go into the bedroom to make your call." Aidan knew that Liam preferred privacy for calls, even if he'd turn around and repeat everything to Aidan.

So Liam did that. The room had a view out to the street, and he watched limousines and taxicabs pass as he waited for the call to connect to Louis in Banneret.

"What kind of trouble have you gotten yourselves into now?" Louis asked.

"You know us so well," Liam said. "At this point we're in over our heads. Let me explain."

He began by paging through the documents, identifying them to Louis. Then he flipped quickly through most of the photos, stopping at several that were graphic pictures of torture, most likely in Evin Prison in Tehran.

"It sounds like you've got some real dynamite there." Louis sighed. "I never had many contacts in the Middle East, and most of the people I knew have either retired or been reassigned. I'll have to make some discreet calls. I can't promise to get back to you today."

"We'll hole up here in the hotel until we hear from you," Liam said. "In the meantime I'll upload the contents of the jump drive." He hung up and opened his laptop. When he, Aidan, Louis, and Hassan opened their business together, they'd established an account with a secure upload site to use when they had to transfer documents.

He set up their VPN ensuring that the connection was safe, then began uploading the documents from the jump drive. It took a while but eventually everything was there, and he sent Louis an email with the password for the files.

Then he walked back to the living room of the suite. "Louis is on the case, but it might take a while."

"What do we do now?"

"We hole up here in this hotel. Order room service, watch TV, play computer games. Wait until Louis gets back to us with some ideas about what we can do with this material."

They called Edwin in and explained the situation. "You think your friend can help?"

"He has in the past." Liam turned to Aidan. "Why don't you tell him about your cousins in Turkey."

Aidan explained how Ellen had recruited them to help cousins on the other side of her family. "Sephardic, like Darius," he said. "Only they were Turkish, living in Istanbul, when they got into trouble."

Liam stood by the window, looking out at the autumn street. He'd forgotten what October was like in the northeast of the US. The oaks and maples were turning shades of gold and red, and he remembered how as a kid he'd raked leaves up and down his street to earn extra money. Then shoveled snow in the winter, dug holes for gardeners in the spring, cut lawns in the summer.

A constant grind to contribute to the house. He hadn't known then that Edwin's father was giving Doris money, and in truth, it probably wasn't enough for the extras that Liam's labors brought in. And then he'd left for the Navy, leaving Doris, Frannie, and Jeannie to fend for themselves.

He pushed those thoughts away and turned back to listen as Aidan told the story of flying to Istanbul and helping the family there come to the United States—carrying a terrible secret. How Louis had been able to use his CIA and State Department contacts to guarantee them safety until they could lure out the bad guys and have them arrested.

"And how are they now?" Edwin asked.

Aidan looked at Liam. "I'm not sure. Like I said, they were what I call collateral cousins—related to my cousin Ellen on the other side of her family. I talk to Ellen every few months but I haven't asked about Yahya and Meryem for a while."

"Why don't you give Ellen a call," Liam said. "As long as we're waiting."

"I can do that." He pulled out his phone and found the speed dial for Ellen Greene. Though she'd married Barry Blattner years before, she'd always kept her maiden name. Aidan smiled to himself. Kind of how he'd kept Greene himself after marrying Liam.

"Hey, cuz," Ellen answered. "How are things in the beautiful French Riviera?"

"Actually, Liam and I are in DC now," he said. "Working for a client. Can I put you on speaker so Liam can hear?"

"Sure. What kind of client? Or can't you say?"

Aidan hit the speaker button. "I'd rather not get into specifics, but we were talking about the Fariases. Our client's late husband was Sephardic, though from Iran."

"Don't get me started on Persian Jews," Ellen said. "A family moved in down the street from us last year, and you would not believe the bling they wear. Though they do have beautiful Persian carpets in every room of the house. They even have small ones hung on the wall in the bathrooms."

Aidan laughed. "Sounds like our client's house in Boca

Raton. But I really wanted to ask you about Yahya and Meriem. How are they?"

"Typical immigrant entrepreneurs," Ellen said. "Within six months, Yahya had a bank loan to buy a run-down building in South Paterson—the area they call Little Istanbul. He renovated it and rented it out to business tenants. Then rinse and repeat. Covid threw his business under the bus for a while but he was smart and under-leveraged so he held on."

"That's great."

"He set Ishak and Havva up in a tiny design studio with a couple of sewing machines, and Ishak has been designing blouses for American women, but with a Turkish flair. Havva started selling them out of the flea market and after six months they opened a retail store on the ground floor of the building."

Aidan looked over at Edwin. "Ishak and Havva are the children, though they must be in their thirties by now."

"You're right," Ellen said. "Havva married a Turkish Jewish guy she met in synagogue, and they have two little children now."

"And Ishak?"

"It took him a while longer, because he was hunched over the sewing machine most of the time. But eventually he fell in love with the UPS driver. He said he couldn't resist a man with his arms full of packages. Demir quit UPS and now he handles all the delivery and logistics for the business."

"That's great. And do they feel... safe?"

"As far as I know. Those guys who were arrested at the funeral were extradited back to Turkey and I don't think there has been any more trouble."

"Thanks, Ellen." He talked with her for a few more

minutes, asking about her husband and their boys. Then he wrapped up the call and turned to Edwin. "So, you see, the last time we needed help from the CIA things worked out fine," he said.

"Let's hope the same thing happens for me," Edwin said.

The three of them sat in the living room and talked for a while, mostly about other branches of Liam's and Edwin's family, people Liam had barely heard of. It made him feel even more isolated to know that Edwin kept in touch with cousins and their children, knew the details of their schooling and careers.

They ordered dinner from room service, and Liam answered the door to the delivery man's knock. He left the chain on and opened the door a fraction. "You can leave the tray there," he said. "We'll get it."

"As you wish," the man said. Liam had a tiny telescope, and he used it to watch the man walk back down the hall to the elevator and then leave. Only then did he open the door and bring the cart in.

He was surprised at the high quality of the food. He'd been expecting burgers and pizza but instead they had shrimp cocktail, steaks, and baked potatoes. "It's nice to have someone else cook for a change, especially when the food is so good," Aidan said.

"I thought you liked to cook," Liam said. Was he oblivious to everything that was going on in his personal life?

"I do. I especially like to cook for you and for our friends. But you know I enjoy eating out, too."

At least Liam knew that. He shook his head. When they got back to Banneret, he really needed to start paying attention to personal stuff.

After dinner, Edwin went into his room to watch TV.

Liam pushed the cart back into the hallway and Aidan called downstairs to say it could be picked up.

Then he and Aidan stayed in the living room. As a SEAL, Liam had mastered the art of waiting. Focus on your breathing, survey your environment, be prepared. Aidan, though, still had work to do on that concept. "Can you please stop pacing?" Liam asked him.

"I'm nervous."

"I understand. I'm worried, too, but the important thing is to keep your guard up. And you can't do that if your mind is obsessed with what might happen."

"I thought that's the way we plan. Think through each possibility and then work out how to succeed."

"It is. But right now we don't have enough information to make any plans."

"Sure we do. One scenario is that the CIA swoops in, takes away the paperwork, and lets us take Edwin back to Boca."

"And what happens when we get back there? How do we let whoever is after Edwin know he doesn't have the materials when we don't even know who they are?"

"Then we do our research." Aidan walked over to the low table and retrieved his laptop. "We look at everything we have, and figure out who could be harmed by releasing it. That gives us a start on who might be after Edwin."

Liam sighed. "You're right, that's a good idea. And it will keep you from wearing a hole in this very expensive rug."

They spent the next couple of hours looking through the materials from the safe deposit box and coming up with some conclusions. Aidan put aside one set of papers. "These pages relate to pro-democracy activists in Tehran and other parts of Iran. Who would want that list?"

"The Iranian government," Liam said. "And maybe one or more other groups who are interested in overthrowing the mullahs. Useful to know who the allies for other teams are."

"Great. That doesn't exactly narrow our focus."

"The evidence of torture is next," Liam said, pointing to another set of papers. "The Iranian government wouldn't want that material released."

"I agree. But if it does get out, the mullahs might be able to establish who leaked the documents. And put that person, or those people, in danger. So maybe the pro-democracy groups don't want that released, at least not yet."

"This is not getting us anywhere," Liam said. "I'm frustrated and irritable."

"I know one way to fix that." Aidan smiled.

"You think sex is always a good fix," Liam grumbled.

"You have anything else to do?"

Liam stood up, already getting hard. "I guess not."

Tuesday morning, they ordered breakfast from room service. Though they'd only been in the hotel less than twenty-four hours, the monotony of their confinement was wearing thin. The knock at the door was a welcome break from the tedium, but Liam knew better than to let his guard down.

He sent Aidan and Edwin into Edwin's bedroom, a precautionary measure that had become routine. With his husband and the client safely out of sight, Liam approached the door, his heart beating a steady rhythm in his chest. He opened the door carefully, keeping the chain latched as an extra layer of security.

A uniformed bellman stood there, his face a mask of

professional courtesy. But something was off. On the cart beside him, there was only a single silver dome covering a plate. Liam's mind raced. There should have been three plates, one for each of them.

Before he could react, the bellman removed the silver cloche with a flourish, revealing not a steaming plate of food, but a pair of metal shears. In a matter of seconds, the bellman cut through the flimsy chain that had been Liam's first line of defense.

Liam's eyes widened as he saw the stout, gray-haired man standing behind the bellman. The man's gun was pointed directly at Liam, unwavering.

"Mr. Grant, I presume," Liam said, his voice steady despite the adrenaline coursing through his veins.

"You have something that belongs to me," Grant replied, his tone flat and emotionless.

Liam's training finally kicked in. In one fluid motion, he used his knee to turn the cart sideways, sending it crashing into the bellman. The rattle of metal and dishes echoed in the narrow hallway, and Liam saw Grant's mouth fall open in surprise.

That split second of distraction was all Liam needed. He slammed the door shut, his fingers fumbling with the bolt and night lock. He knew that the flimsy hotel locks wouldn't hold for long, but every second counted.

With the door secure, Liam jumped to the side, pressing his back against the wall. His heart hammered in his chest as he waited for the inevitable sound of gunshots. He doubted that Grant would be brash enough to have his man shoot through the door, but in his line of work, taking chances was a luxury he couldn't afford.

Chapter 23

Ball-Stretcher

Liam

Grant spoke through the door. "This isn't over. I'll be back."

"Yeah, you and Arnold Schwarzenegger," Liam said. He listened carefully, but couldn't tell if Grant and his henchman were still outside.

Aidan came out of the bedroom then. "What was all the clatter? And where's breakfast?"

"Small complication," Liam said, waving him to the side. He left the wall, careful to stay out of the line of fire if gunshots came through the door. In a low voice, he explained what had happened.

Aidan tried to walk over to the door, but Liam pulled him back. "He could still be out there," he said.

Aidan looked at the chain and shook his head. "Edwin's going to have to pay for that." He turned back to Liam. "You think we should call Louis again? Update him?"

"I'm sure he understands the urgency. But now that we know for sure Grant is a bad guy we should probably tell Louis."

Before he could do so, though, Liam's phone rang from

an unknown number. "What do you think? Grant?" he asked Aidan.

Aidan shrugged. "Only one way to find out."

Liam thumbed the phone. "Hello."

"Does the phrase ball-stretcher mean anything to you?"

Liam laughed, and some of the fear he'd been feeling faded away. Years ago, during the problems with the Farias family, Louis had connected them with an active CIA officer named Joel Serrano. That was the code phrase they'd used back then. "Officer Serrano?"

"In the flesh. Actually, outside the hotel. If you come to the window you can see me."

Liam walked over to the window that looked out at the street. Serrano was there, and Liam waved. "Glad you're here. Come on up. But be careful." He explained how Harvey Grant had come to the door earlier, and that he might still be around.

"I know Mr. Grant," Serrano said. "And I know how to avoid being seen."

Liam hung up the phone. "The cavalry is here. That was Joel Serrano, and he's on his way up."

"Do we know we can trust him?" Aidan asked. "After all, Grant was part of the State Department."

"He remembered the code we used the last time we met," Liam said. "At this point I don't know what else we can do."

Edwin came out of his bedroom. "Breakfast here?"

"Give us a couple of minutes," Liam said.

He looked back out at the street. Serrano was gone, most likely on his way up to the hotel room. His phone rang again, once more from an unknown number.

"I'm in the hall," Serrano said. "The area is clear."

Liam walked over and opened the door by a few inches.

Serrano was there, apparently alone except for a cart with three domes on it. "I brought breakfast," Serrano said. "Found this abandoned down the hall."

"Come on in," Liam said.

"Oh, good, breakfast." Edwin reached into his pocket for a bill. "Thank you."

Liam and Aidan laughed as Serrano pushed the cart into the room. Liam locked the door behind him and threw the bolt. "This is Officer Joel Serrano of the CIA," Liam said. "You don't need to tip him."

Edwin looked confused. "You'll catch up," Aidan said.

They all sat at the table in the living room and Aidan put out the food. "Have a cinnamon roll," Aidan said to Serrano. "I ordered extra because I figured it would be a long day."

"Quite possibly," Serrano said, as he took the roll. "But not at this hotel, now that Grant knows you're here. And that presents another problem, because he probably knows most if not all the safe houses we have in the area."

As they ate, Aidan leaned over to Edwin and filled him in. Liam noticed his cousin's face get paler as he understood.

"Any idea why Grant turned?" Liam asked Serrano.

"Harvey Grant was a big shot at State, and he left under a cloud, because he differed with the administration on how to handle the Iran situation. He's never been a big fan of either the shah or the mullahs, and he was always pushing for funding for the pro-democracy factions. I'm guessing that his ego got the upper hand when he was kicked to the curb."

He frowned. "There was also a rumor that he was selling confidential information to wealthy Iranian expats. But there was no official investigation."

Aidan poured coffee for the four of them. "How did Darius come into this?" Edwin asked. "One of those wealthy Iranian expats?"

Serrano nodded. "I believe Grant saw Mr. Ashoori as a man with deep pockets with a personal interest in Iran. I ran my own check on the bank account you sent Louis, and I can confirm that money was going to a group Grant controls. And that part of the money was siphoned off into Grant's personal account."

"Do you think he assembled the file Darius was holding?" Liam asked.

"I don't know. It's possible Grant needed a safe place to stash the material, not connected to him. If that's the case, then giving Darius the material to hold was a way of bringing him into the cause."

"Can't we give it back to him and put all this behind us?" Edwin asked. "God knows I have no vested interest in what happens in Iran. I've never even been there. And given that I know Darius was lying to me, I'm less inclined to put myself in danger because of something foolish he did."

Serrano sipped his coffee. "I'll have to look through what you've got very carefully. Grant is a private citizen now, so there's no reason for him to be the custodian of information that could damage national security as well as upend the balance of power in Iran."

"You'll find there is material there that supports all sides of the conflict," Liam said. "Abuses by the shah's people, back in the day, and by the mullahs today. Even the pro-democracy folks have a few skeletons in their closet."

"This is dangerous stuff," Serrano said. "If there's a leak at State it needs to be plugged. And people at a much higher pay grade than mine will need to be notified."

He finished his cinnamon roll. "Now if you'll excuse me, I need to find a place where I can take you." He stood and walked into the bedroom Edwin had been using, closing the door behind him.

"You know, ever since I got that call from the police that Darius had been killed, my primary emotion has been sadness," Edwin said. "But now anger is beginning to overpower that. How dare Darius do this to me? It's stupid enough that he risked his own life for people half a world away, but now I'm in danger, too, and I've brought you into my trouble."

"You did the smart thing," Liam said.

"If I'd been smart, I'd have known what Darius was up to and put a stop to it."

Edwin sat on the sofa and busied himself with his phone. Aidan cleaned up, and Liam thought about how they could best protect Edwin. That was their job. Serrano was there to protect the interests of the United States government, and Liam knew that while he wouldn't unnecessarily put Edwin in danger, protecting the client was not his highest priority.

It was Aidan's and Liam's though. And not only because Edwin was paying them, but because he had to admit that he'd begun to develop a family feeling for his cousin.

Serrano emerged from Edwin's room. "I've got some plans," he said. "I've found a safe house where I can take you. It recently came under agency purview, so it's doubtful Grant knows about it. And even if he does, it's out in the country and very defensible."

"We haven't unpacked much," Aidan said. "I can have us ready to leave in about ten minutes."

"I'll need more time to get a convoy in place," Serrano said. "Let's say we depart here at eleven hundred."

Edwin went into his room to pack, and Aidan did the same. "What's the plan after we get to this safe house?" Liam asked Serrano.

"We need to flush out whoever is interested in this material," Serrano said. "Grant certainly, but there may be others. So our plan right now is to set up a handoff. We give Grant the material in a public way, so that anyone who is watching knows to go after him rather than your client."

"And then you arrest Grant?"

"That's going to be tricky. It is illegal under Federal law to remove classified material with the intent to hold it. But we'd have to prove that Grant was the one who removed the material in the first place. That's possible but it's going to take some time to investigate, and we'd rather move quickly and arrest later."

"Will that lift the threat to Edwin?"

"Again, I can't promise anything yet, because we don't know who else is interested in what's in that folder, and that makes it hard to prove that your client hasn't held anything back."

Serrano walked over to the table. "Now, if you please, let's look through what you've got."

They verified that the jump drive contained digital copies of everything on paper. Then Serrano looked through the material, page by page, as Aidan and eventually Edwin joined them in the living room.

Aidan kept Edwin engaged in a corner of the room. As far as Liam could tell they were talking about Edwin's childhood, and his few encounters with Liam—or Billy, as he was called then.

At eleven o'clock, Serrano's phone rang. "Vehicle is

outside," he said. "Additional officers will be here in minutes to guard you all until you're safe in the vehicle."

"Aidan and I don't need officers to guard us," Liam said.

"Let's establish one thing before we go forward," Serrano said, in a very pleasant voice. "I'm in charge of this operation, and you and your partner and your client follow my orders to keep you safe."

Liam chafed at that, but he nodded. "Understood. But I'll drive our rental car. We don't want to abandon it here at the hotel."

Serrano gave Liam the address of the house, which he plugged into his phone's map application. A young red-headed officer came to the door, and Aidan, Liam and Edwin hoisted their bags and followed him and Serrano, down the hall, down the stairs, to the lobby. The manager stood by the front desk. "You have my credit card," Edwin said to him. "Charge me what you need to."

"Be careful, Mr. Gallagher."

Edwin nodded, and the three of them followed the officers out to a black Lincoln Navigator parked in the loading zone in front of the hotel. Another officer by the SUV waved an all-clear signal to Serrano, and Aidan climbed in as Liam stowed their luggage in the back.

"I'll meet you at the safe house," Liam said to Edwin.

"You're not riding with us?"

"Aidan will take care of you," Liam said.

Chapter 24

Last Words

Liam

By the time Liam had retrieved their rented SUV from the hotel garage, the officers had left. As he slid behind the wheel, he took a moment to steady his breathing and gather his thoughts. The weight of his decisions pressed down on him, and he couldn't shake the feeling that he was walking a tightrope without a net.

He dutifully followed the directions his phone gave him, his mind racing as he navigated the unfamiliar streets. He couldn't help but wonder if Serrano had been straight with him. The man had seemed genuine enough, but in Liam's line of work, trust was a commodity that couldn't be given lightly.

If Serrano was operating on his own agenda, if this was all some sort of trap, then Liam had put both Aidan and Edwin in danger. The thought made his stomach churn, and he gripped the steering wheel until his knuckles turned white. He had sworn to protect his cousin, to keep him safe from the dangers that lurked in the shadows of his husband's past. But now, he had willingly sent his husband and his client off with a government operative, trusting that Serrano's officers would keep them out of harm's way.

He took the 14th Street Bridge over the Potomac, passing the Pentagon. He'd been in what was now the world's second-biggest office building on only one occasion, when his team received a briefing before they left on an operation. He had little memory of the place—they'd been shuttled into a meeting room, their movements carefully controlled. Then they'd been taken to a government airfield where they'd boarded a transport.

He didn't like being put back in that position, where he could not control the information surrounding his operation. It was hard ceding that to Joel Serrano, even if he'd come through in the past.

He continued southwest on 395 into Virginia. After following a convoluted cloverleaf he was on the Capital Beltway heading back toward DC, but quickly exited at Claremont Drive. He navigated a series of local roads until he pulled up at an impressive brick two-story house on a large lot at the end of a street.

He was relieved to see the agency SUV and another sedan in the driveway. He parked to one side and walked up to Serrano. "If you listen, you can hear the highway from here, but there isn't easy access," Serrano said. "For the rendezvous, we'll need an open area without the possibility of getting citizens involved." He smiled. "No cemeteries convenient."

The last time they'd organized something like this, the takedown had occurred at a cemetery in New Jersey. Good to see that Serrano had such a strong memory.

Serrano waved his hand toward the woods beyond the house. "There's a small park at the end of the street, around the bend. Nobody ever goes there, but we'll have officers clear the area just in case. Then we'll have a SWAT team hidden in the trees at the time of the rendezvous."

"When do you want to do this?" Liam asked.

"Sooner is better, but we want all parties to know what's going down and have time to react. Most likely tomorrow morning if the weather holds."

It was cool and in the high sixties, with a bright sun. The trees in the nearby woods were a mix of evergreen and deciduous, and reminded Liam of childhood days spent roaming the woods at the edge of New Brunswick, picking up colored leaves and pinecones. He and a friend had heard that cones made a good fire, and gone to the friend's house to light one.

Unfortunately they hadn't realized there was a damper on the chimney so they hadn't opened it, and the friend's house had filled with smoke. Liam had taken a beating for that from Big Bill.

Not a memory he wanted to cherish.

Serrano led them inside, followed by the red-haired junior officer, whose name was Gardner. With Edwin by his side, Aidan organized bedrooms and put together a meal order. Meanwhile Serrano, Gardner and Liam inspected the whole property and talked through what they'd do. Eventually they sat at a picnic table in the back yard.

"We want to use the least secure channel to convey the information to Grant," Serrano said. "Probably your client's cell phone. We want anyone who wants to know to be able to hear the details."

"You still believe there's someone else besides Grant who wants this information?" Liam asked.

"Grant is a diplomat, so his first goal is going to be negotiation," Serrano said. "That doesn't fit with the shooting of Mr. Ashoori. That was intimidation, and if the goal was to get Ashoori to give up the dossier, it was stupid. Grant is not stupid."

"That means someone else killed Darius. Why?" Liam noticed that the junior officer spoke only when Serrano asked him a question. He was probably in his late twenties or early thirties, only a couple of years out of Camp Peary, the "Farm" where CIA officers were trained.

"What do you think?" Serrano asked Liam.

"Maybe the person behind the shooter knew about the money Darius was sending, and wanted to shut that off. Didn't know about the dossier."

"That's what I think. Then you had three burglary attempts at the house in Boca."

Liam nodded. "We assumed the burglars were looking for the dossier, or the key to the safe deposit box."

"Which means the burglars knew about the dossier. That draws a line from them to Grant, a line that doesn't connect to the shooting."

"Meaning two different groups."

"At least two. There are currently six active political groups inside Iran, ranging from religious to liberal to social democratic. Then outside the country you have monarchist groups and ethnic groups. Any one of them would love to get their hands on this material."

"When we were researching Grant's group, the Organization for a Democratic Persia, we came up with another one, the Iranian Defense Force. Know anything about them?"

"The IDF are a group of Iranian nationals living in the US who support the mullahs. We've had them under surveillance for some time. They're suspected in a couple of minor crimes, like interfering with demonstrations or harassing other Iranian nationals who don't agree with them."

"That's all? No criminal records?"

"If we had evidence, we'd deport them."

"But they could be spying on Grant and his operation," Liam suggested. "They might know what's in the dossier, or at least that the dossier exists. Once Darius was killed, that set off a scramble."

"You should be in politics," Serrano said.

Liam shook his head. "I like being my own boss, as much as possible."

"And you've got a good partner. I've seen the way you two work. Aidan's Mr. Inside, managing the client, and you're Mr. Outside."

"For the most part. When we need to, we work together. For example, Aidan's a crack shot, even better than I am. Which reminds me, will you arm us? We obviously couldn't bring weapons with us from France."

"I can get you Glock 19s. You familiar with those?"

Liam nodded. "We use them in France."

He moved over to Liam's side of the picnic bench and pulled out a pocket notebook. He and Serrano composed a simple message to text to Harvey Grant. As Grant suspected, they were in possession of a dossier and a jump drive with information Grant would be interested in. They'd trade it for a guarantee that Edwin would be safe.

Then Liam went into the house and found Aidan and Edwin in the living room. "May I have your phone, please?" he asked his cousin.

"Sure." Edwin handed it to him. "What's going on?"

"We're sending a text message to Harvey Grant about a rendezvous tomorrow." He didn't bother to add they hoped others might be listening in, especially the IDF.

The Designer of His Own Fortune

When he returned outside, Serrano had sent Gardner off on errands. The CIA officer checked a sophisticated weather app on his phone. "Partly cloudy tomorrow morning, no chance of rain. I say we go for eleven o'clock."

Liam typed the message into Edwin's phone and hit 'send.' Then they waited.

"Let's hope if there are other actors they're tapping Grant's phone or your cousin's," Serrano said. He leaned forward and rested his elbows on the picnic table. "My job isn't usually this lively. Most of the time I'm in the office reviewing documents and going to meetings. I brought Gardner along because this will be good experience for him."

"He seems so young," Liam said.

"Don't let his age fool you. He was tops in his class at The Farm, he has a photographic memory, and he processes information like a computer."

Liam looked at his phone and noticed the dots below his message that indicated Grant was responding. "Incoming," he said, and he and Serrano hunched over the phone.

The dots disappeared. Then they returned again. "What's he writing, *War and Peace?*" Liam grumbled.

Eventually two letters appeared. OK. Then more dots. "Will need to verify contents of the dossier and the drive."

Serrano nodded, and Liam typed OK back at Grant.

"Now we wait." They walked inside and Serrano sat at the dining room table. He opened his laptop and Liam assumed he went back to his other operations.

Liam climbed the stairs to the second floor and found Aidan in the house's master bedroom. "Where's Edwin?"

"Room next door," Aidan said. "This is all starting to wear on him. He's like a piece of china, ready to break at any moment."

"He's going to have to hold it together another twenty-four hours." Liam told Aidan about the text to Grant, and the meeting the next morning. Then he shook out his arms. "I'm antsy. Want to go for a run but I don't know this neighborhood and I don't want to expose myself to anything."

"There's an exercise bike in the study down the hall," Aidan said. "Knock yourself out."

It wasn't like riding through the foothills of the Alpes Maritimes around Banneret, but Liam made do. It was a fancy model with an internet connection, and he could have figured out how the program worked and set up a virtual route. But all he wanted to do was put his head down and ride until he worked off his anxiety. By the time he'd biked, showered, and dressed again, Gardner returned with an overnight bag, two medium pizzas and bottles of soda and 10 PH water.

"My body's forming kidney stones," Serrano said, as he took the water bottle. "My urologist has me on this water to reduce the acidity."

"I'll take some of that," Aidan said. "I had a kidney stone last year. Miserable pain when it started to move."

Liam looked at his husband. The kidney stone drama had been a reminder that both were getting older, and that it might be something biological that killed them rather than a bullet from a bad guy.

"Officer Gardner will stay here with you tonight, and I'll be back in the morning," Serrano said, as they ate.

Aidan turned to the young redhead. "So, Officer Gardner, tell us something about yourself. Since we're going to be housemates tonight. You have a first name?"

Serrano laughed. "Great opening question. Tell them your full name."

Gardner frowned at his boss. "Woodrow Wilson Gardner the third," he said. "But you can call me Will."

"Never Woody," Serrano said.

"That's my dad."

"I grew up being called Billy or Little Bill," Liam said. "My dad was Big Bill. I decided when I left the Navy I'd switch to Liam, but my full name is William."

He didn't add that part of the reason he changed his name was because he stepped out of the closet and wanted to put away lying and hiding, along with that name.

Aidan looked at Gardner. "Anything else you'd like to share?"

"Yale undergrad. Master's in Diplomatic Studies from Oxford. First in my class at The Farm."

"Why the CIA?" Aidan asked. "Not the State Department?"

"I wouldn't be opposed to a position OCONUS with State," Gardner said. "But I wanted to learn from the ground up."

"Oconus?" Edwin asked.

"Acronym," Liam said. "Outside the Continental United States. Kind of like the one for Agents Navigating for the United States."

"ANUS," Aidan said, and all of them laughed except Edwin.

"That isn't a real acronym, is it?" Edwin asked.

"You never know," Serrano said. "The United States government is a cesspool of acronyms. My favorite is from a bill sponsored by Senator Tester of Montana." He spelled out the letters in the word PROSTATE. "Stands for the Prostate Research, Outreach, Screening, Testing, Access, and Treatment Effectiveness Act."

"His name really isn't Tester, is it?" Edwin asked.

"Indeed it is," Serrano said. "Jon Tester, of the Big Sky Country."

They talked and laughed for a while and then Serrano announced he was leaving. "You're in good hands here. I'll be back tomorrow morning and we'll run some rehearsals for the handoff. In the meantime, I'll take the dossier and the drive with me and get them copied."

"You said you could provide us with weapons," Liam said.

"Will has them," Serrano said.

He left, and Gardner retrieved his overnight bag, which contained two Glock 19s as well as extra ammunition. "You're familiar with these?" he asked.

"They're what we use in France." Liam took one gun and Aidan the other, and they both checked to make sure they were unloaded, then examined them closely.

"This is making me nervous," Edwin said.

"You won't be involved in the handoff," Liam said. "I'm going to take care of that. Aidan will stay behind with you. And I'll have officers hidden around me to protect me. There's nothing to be nervous about."

Famous last words, he thought. He hoped they wouldn't be among his last words.

Chapter 25

I Will Survive
Aidan

When Aidan was confident his gun was ready to use, he looked over at Edwin. The client's hands shook and there were dark circles beneath his eyes, despite the number of hours he'd ostensibly been napping or sleeping.

Gardner stood up. "If the guns pass muster with you, I'll excuse myself. "I've got some work to do."

He left, and Aidan, Liam and Edwin remained in the living room. "This has been a tough ten days for you," Aidan said to Edwin.

"Like an awful, never-ending roller coaster ride," Edwin said. "All twists and turns and steep descents." He sighed. "I used to complain to Darius that our lives were so dull. Restaurants, shopping, charitable functions. I missed the excitement of New York. Now I realize Darius had his own action movie playing in his mind, and I didn't even play a part in it."

"I'd love to hear more about your life in New York," Aidan said, settling back against the sofa cushions. He looked at his husband. "Liam, I saw some hot chocolate packets in the kitchen cabinet. You think you could make some for us?"

Though Liam usually left the cooking to him, Aidan knew his husband would be more comfortable rattling around the kitchen than hearing Edwin's stories.

"Absolutely." Liam rose with his typical grace and walked toward the kitchen. Aidan couldn't help admiring his butt as he walked, and it appeared Edwin did, too.

"I never had a figure like that," Edwin said, when Liam was out of the room.

"Believe me, he works for it," Aidan said. "You know he was a Navy SEAL, right?"

"Aunt Doris said he was in the Navy. I thought he was a regular sailor."

Aidan shook his head. "Liam never settles for being a regular anything. He's told me how he started working out in high school to be able to defend himself against his father."

"Did Uncle Bill beat him?" Edwin asked, his mouth agape.

"I think it was more like a threat, especially as Liam got older and bigger. But he was also working out some things in his brain, as you can imagine."

"Was he out in the military?"

Aidan shook his head. "He was conflicted for a long time. The whole Catholic thing, and I guess the nature of who he was attracted to."

"Not queeny men like Darius and me."

"No. I had some of the same issues, growing up. You know, wanting a big strong man to hug me. I knew a few men with overtly homosexual mannerisms and I didn't want anything to do with them."

"Afraid they'd reveal your secret," Edwin said.

"Exactly."

"I was lucky, landing in the fashion business in 1982," Edwin said. "Well, lucky in one way, extraordinarily unlucky in another."

Aidan leaned forward to encourage him to continue.

"We started hearing about the gay cancer soon after I got into the business," Edwin said. "At first it was only in the news, but then men I worked with started getting sick. Spots, throat infections. We tried to ignore it as long as possible, but when men started dying you couldn't anymore."

Aidan felt lucky that in 1982, he'd only been eight years old. Old enough to have stirrings of strange feelings but protected from the disease that was ravaging the gay community.

Edwin sighed. "I went to so many funerals back then. And not only did it affect me personally, but at work, too. I was constantly scrambling to find people to fill positions. It was like a cyclone came through, taking away employees and contractors with hardly a moment's notice."

Aidan heard Liam moving around the kitchen, glad his husband was missing this. "You know, people don't talk about it much, but a lot of straight women died then, too," Edwin said. "Men who were in the closet were infecting their wives and girlfriends. We had a room of seamstresses from Puerto Rico and the Dominican Republic, and they were dying, too."

"And in the middle of that you met Darius," Aidan said. He'd hoped for stories of glittering parties, but it if helped Edwin to talk, he'd listen.

"I met Darius," Edwin said. "I was such a drab person then. Trying to distance myself. Men I knew wore denim and leather and brightly colored shirts but I kept to standard

Brooks Brothers drag. I thought if I wore dark suits and white shirts and spit-shined loafers I'd be safe."

"Darius must have seen something in you, underneath," Aidan said.

"He was fastidious about his health, even back then," Edwin said. "As soon as he learned how you could catch the disease he started taking precautions. Hand jobs, frottage, and condoms even for blow jobs. That, and our quick commitment to monogamy, saved us."

He started to cry again. "But it didn't matter in the end, did it? Darius is dead and I'm on my own."

Liam walked in carrying a tray loaded with three mugs of hot chocolate and he cast a disapproving glance at Aidan, as if to say, 'this is how you're cheering up the client?'

He set the tray down on the coffee table and handed a mug to Edwin. "Aidan says chocolate always makes things better."

Edwin dried his eyes with a white handkerchief. "Aidan is a wise man. You're lucky to have found him."

"We're both lucky," Aidan said. "But come on, you were going to tell me about parties. Did you ever go to Studio 54?"

"We did. It was as wild as you've heard, especially in the private rooms in the basement. Darius wouldn't use drugs, and he'd certainly never have sex in public, so we didn't get up to the kind of things some people did. Mostly we stood around holding drinks and talking to people, though occasionally we danced."

"What's your favorite song to dance to?" Aidan asked.

"I Will Survive," Edwin said, without hesitation. "Gloria Gaynor was the diva of the moment, and every time that song came on Darius would tug me out to the dance floor and we'd let go."

Aidan grabbed his phone and opened Apple Music. He started the song and turned up the volume, then stood up. "Come on, let's dance."

"I couldn't," Edwin said. "It's been a long time."

Aidan leaned down and tugged on his arm. "It's like riding a bicycle," he said. "You don't forget."

"Aidan," Liam said. "If he doesn't want to dance..."

"All right." Edwin stood up, stepped away from the coffee table, and swung his hips experimentally. "You're right, it comes back to you," he said. "But if I break a hip, it's on you."

He began moving his arms to the beat and swiveling his body, and Aidan saw the moment when the music overtook him. He began dancing, too, trying to experience that same out-of-body moment. His head moved from side to side and he grinned. "Come on, Liam. Don't be an old fuddy-duddy."

Liam remained on the sofa with his arms crossed. Aidan looked over at the doorway to the living room and saw Will Gardner there. "Is this a private dance party or can anyone join?" he asked.

"Come on in," Aidan said, turning his body to welcome the young man.

Liam wasn't the jealous type, but Aidan knew that eventually he wouldn't want to be left out. Despite the grace with which he moved, he wasn't a very good dancer—he'd spent all those years in the closet when other young men were learning their moves.

Will Gardner, though, was a pro, sliding his feet, turning, and rocking, and the four of them danced as Aidan put the song on repeat. It was a good anthem for them—no matter what happened the next day, they'd all survive. Or at least Aidan hoped so.

Chapter 26

Unknown

Liam

Wednesday morning Joel Serrano returned with donuts and coffee, and the five of them sat in the kitchen and talked about what would happen that day. "My team is already getting in place," he said. "How do you want to handle the actual handoff?"

"I'll do it," Liam said. "Grant already knows me, and I don't want to put Edwin in danger. He'll stay in the house with Aidan."

"Sounds good."

Serrano and Gardner were busy on their phones and laptops, while Liam and Aidan spent the morning in the house's study, which had big windows overlooking the back yard. Aidan stood there beside Edwin, trying to distract himself and the client by looking for birds. "A cardinal!" he said, his voice a little too cheerful. "And those black ones with the forked tails are grackles."

"It has been a long time since I've seen birds like these," Edwin said. "In Florida, we get egrets and cranes and the occasional roseate spoonbill." He peered out the window, his brow furrowing. "Look up there at the top of the tree. Is that an owl?"

Liam thought it was good to keep them involved in something other than thinking about the upcoming handoff, and the possibility that the threat against Edwin would be lifted. "Why don't I get our binoculars," he said.

He went up to the room he and Aidan were sharing, his footsteps heavy on the stairs. When he found the binoculars they felt cold and heavy in his hands. Before heading back downstairs, he walked over to the window and looked out. It took some scanning and focusing, but he brought the owl into view, watching as it swooped down to catch an errant mouse, lifting it in its claws.

He took the binoculars downstairs and handed them to his cousin, forcing a smile. He was glad to have spared Edwin that glimpse into the danger that lurked beyond the safety of the house.

At half-past ten, Serrano came into the study. "Let's get out to the park," he said. Liam felt his heart rate quicken, a sense of unease settling in the pit of his stomach. He glanced at Aidan and Edwin, seeing the same apprehension reflected in their eyes. They all knew that this was no ordinary outing, that the park held more than just trees and trails.

As he and Serrano prepared to leave, Liam couldn't shake the feeling that they were walking into the lion's den. But he steeled himself, knowing that there was no turning back now. They had come too far, risked too much, to give up.

Liam pulled Aidan aside. "I want to be able to leave as soon as we can. Get packed and wait in the kitchen until I call. Then we hop into the SUV and get the hell out of here."

"Will do," Aidan said.

As Liam settled into the passenger seat of Serrano's agency car, he felt a mix of anticipation and trepidation. He watched carefully as Serrano backed out of the driveway, his eyes tracking every movement, every turn. The weight of the situation pressed down on him, and he couldn't shake the feeling that they were heading into uncharted territory.

The car turned left, and Liam's mind raced with possibilities. What would happen at the park? Would Grant be there, accept the file, and drive away? Or would he come with reinforcements, try and eliminate Liam, with the intent of doing the same to Aidan and Edwin?

As they circled around the wooded area adjacent to the house, Liam's thoughts drifted to Aidan and Edwin. He hated leaving them behind, even if it was for their own safety. The thought of something happening to them while he was gone made his chest tighten with fear. There were other groups involved in this problem, and perhaps the IDF, or someone else, would go after Edwin with only Aidan there to protect him.

He had to focus on the task at hand, to trust that Serrano knew what he was doing, that he had a plan. Still, the uncertainty gnawed at him, and he found himself clenching his fists, his nails digging into his palms.

The car pulled into the park a few minutes later, and Liam's heart rate quickened. This was it, the moment of truth. He took a deep breath, trying to steady his nerves. As he stared at the woods ahead of him, he felt a sense of determination.

Grant was nothing, in the end. An old man with a heightened sense of his own importance. Liam could face him easily.

At five minutes before eleven, Serrano's phone rang and

he answered through his headset. "We have eyes on Grant," he said to Liam. "He should be here right on time."

"Anyone else in the area?"

"Only my team."

Liam plugged his own earpiece in, and Serrano opened a call to him. "Hearing you loud and clear," Liam said.

Serrano handed him the folder and the jump drive. "Everything has been copied to my team," he said.

Liam's pulse raced as he got out of the car, but he forced himself to be calm. This was like any of the operations he'd participated in during his time as a SEAL. Handoff the folder and the drive, then hotfoot it back to Serrano's car.

A late model Mercedes pulled into the parking lot, its sleek black exterior gleaming in the sunlight. Liam watched as it came to a stop, his heart pounding in his chest. He held up the folder in one hand and the jump drive in the other, a silent signal to the car's occupant.

Taking a deep breath, Liam began walking toward the Mercedes, his footsteps echoing in the otherwise quiet park. Each step felt like a lifetime, the distance between him and the car stretching out before him like an endless expanse.

As he approached, the driver's side door opened, and Grant stepped out, wearing the kind of suit he probably dressed in every day at the State Department. The man's face was a mask of smug satisfaction, his eyes glinting with a hint of malice. "I'm glad you saw reason," he called out, his voice carrying across the distance between them.

Liam opened his mouth to respond, but before he could utter a word, the roar of another engine shattered the stillness. He turned, his eyes widening as a big Toyota SUV came barreling into the park, gravel scattering in its wake. The vehicle screeched to a halt, and two men with AR-15s jumped out, their weapons at the ready.

"What the!" Grant exclaimed, his face contorting in a mixture of surprise and anger.

"You are all traitors to Islam!" one man said, his accent heavy.

Before Liam could respond, shots began to ring out, the sound deafening in the confined space of the parking lot. Liam instinctively ducked, his heart racing as bullets whizzed past him, kicking up dirt and leaves as they struck the ground.

He glanced around, desperately searching for cover. Was the SWAT engaging the newcomers? Or had Grant pulled a gun to protect what he thought was his?

He had to act fast, had to get to safety. Without a second thought, Liam darted for the woods, his legs pumping as he ran in a zigzag pattern. Bullets continued to fly, hitting the dirt around him, but he didn't dare look back. He focused on the shelter of the trees ahead, his breath coming in ragged gasps as he pushed himself to the limit.

As he reached the woods, Liam kept running, the sound of gunfire fading behind him. His mind raced, trying to make sense of what had just happened. Who were those men? Why had they shown up now, of all times?

He shook his head, knowing that he didn't have time to dwell on those questions. He had to keep moving, had to get in touch with Aidan. Reaching up to his headset, he gasped out, "Hey, Siri, call Aidan."

As the phone began to ring, Liam pressed on, his heart pounding in his ears. He could only hope that Aidan would answer, that he was safe. The thought of losing him, of losing everything he had fought so hard for, was too much to bear.

"We're ready to go," Aidan said when he answered.

"Good. Get in the SUV now and start the engine. I'm on my way."

"What about..." Aidan began, but Liam ended the call and focused on the run through the woods. He had to head northeast to get back to the house, and from the position of the sun through the treetops he adjusted his direction.

It seemed to take forever, but was probably only five minutes before he reached the edge of the trees. He looked left and right. The only vehicle in the area was their SUV, positioned in the driveway for a quick exit. He dashed across the lawn and jumped in the passenger side.

Aidan had the SUV going before Liam could even close the door. He leaned inside and slammed it shut. "Back to the highway," he said. "Left at the end of the street, then take the second right."

Liam's phone rang. "Serrano? What happened?"

"Unknown intervention," Serrano said. "Both shooters are down, but Grant got away. Where are you?"

"We'll be in touch," Liam said, and ended the call.

"Where are we going once we hit the highway?" Aidan asked.

"Haven't thought that far ahead. Things went to hell back there at the park. Two guys pulled up in an SUV with AR-15s and started shooting. I managed to duck into the park and left Serrano and his team to handle things."

"You didn't give Grant the folder or the drive?" Edwin asked from the back seat.

Liam twisted around to face him. "Didn't have a chance."

"So he's going to keep coming after me." Edwin slumped back against the seat.

"I believe so. But the good news is that we flushed out

the other group. According to Serrano both shooters went down. It's possible that one of them killed Darius."

Aidan came to the highway entrance. "Which way?"

"I don't want to go back to DC. We need to go to ground for a while until we can give Serrano time to figure things out and we can decide on our own how we move forward."

"Short Hills," Edwin said.

Aidan turned east on the highway. "Excuse me?"

"My cousin Mary Elizabeth. You met her at the funeral. She has a house in Short Hills, not far from where I grew up. She's in Florida for the winter, so we can hide out there. Big piece of property, state-of-the-art alarm system. Five bedrooms, which I've been telling her she doesn't need, but she likes to have her kids and grandkids come to visit when she's there."

Aidan turned to Liam. "How does that sound?"

"Works for me. I'll get you directions."

Liam plugged the address into his phone while Edwin called Mary Elizabeth to make sure it was all right to use the house. He spoke to her for a minute or two. "Thank you so much, sweetheart. Don't worry, we're fine. I want to get away from all the drama in Boca and avoid thinking about Darius for a while."

He ended the call. "Her next-door neighbor has the key. She's emailing me the alarm codes."

Liam turned to Aidan. "95 north all the way up through Jersey to exit eleven, when we turn onto the Garden State."

"We're going right past exit nine," Aidan said. "New Brunswick. Your home ground."

"Don't remind me," Liam said as they headed farther into the unknown.

Chapter 27

Trader Joe's

Aidan

As they drove, Aidan listened to Liam's phone ring three more times, and each time he refused the call. "When are you going to talk to Serrano?"

"When he's had time to process what went on. Before that all he's going to want to know is where we are and what we're doing. And I don't want to tell him."

Once they got out of the sprawl of the District of Columbia and its environs, the highway took on a familiar lull. Aidan's father was a collector of antique guns, and as a kid his family had traveled to Washington yearly for a big gun show. His father would talk about Civil War weapons, his specialty, while Aidan and his mother walked around and looked at vendor tables.

Each year, he got to pick out a rabbit skin, and he had a collection of them in different shades, from black to mottled brown and white, to pure white. The fur was soft and the skins a pebbled tan, and he never bothered to think they had come from a live animal. He wondered sometimes if his ability to shoot was genetic, passed from his father, who used to go out to the railyard of Newark as a teen to shoot rats.

However he'd come by it, it was a useful talent to have in his current occupation. He'd never known he was that good until he took that short course in personal protection after deciding to work with Liam. His instructors had been awed by his ability, as had Liam.

He recognized many of the exits and rest stops. They'd had to stop at the Chesapeake House travel plaza when his mother's car began acting up, and had to wait for a mechanic to arrive and repair the alternator. They'd passed Elkton once and his mother told him it was a place for quickie marriages, where there was no need for blood tests or a waiting period.

He was so caught up in his memories that they were in mid-Jersey before he snapped out. "I remember as a kid they hadn't extended 95 out here yet," he said, as they passed the exit for I-195 west and Trenton. "If we wanted to go to New York, we had to take US 1 all the way up to New Brunswick to catch the Turnpike."

"About the only thing New Brunswick had going for it. Well, that and Rutgers," Liam said.

"You never wanted to go to college?" Edwin asked from the back seat.

"My high school guidance counselor wanted me to apply," Liam said. "She said I had the grades. But I wanted to get out of the house, and the campus was too close. I opted for the Navy instead."

"You know it's only about forty-five minutes from Short Hills to New Brunswick," Edwin said. "While we're waiting for Mr. Serrano, we could visit Aunt Doris."

"Not likely," Liam said.

"Your mother would be hurt to know you were so close and didn't stop by," Edwin said.

"Who's going to tell her? Not me."

"Think about it, Liam," Aidan said. "You know I'm not Doris's biggest fan, but she's your mother. And who knows, maybe her association with Edwin has softened her up toward gay people."

"If it makes you feel any better she hasn't used the word fairy or faggot to me for years," Edwin said.

Liam laughed. "That's a ringing endorsement."

He crossed his arms over his chest, and Aidan knew that meant no more discussion of the topic. But once they had put New Brunswick in their rear-view mirror, each of them noticed something on the road worth mentioning. "My high school prom was in a banquet hall at this exit," Liam said.

"You went to your prom?" Edwin asked. "With a girl?"

"Boys weren't taking boys to prom back then," Liam said drily. "Not that I would have been a pioneer even if it was possible."

"I didn't go to my prom," Edwin said. "Pingry had been an all-boys school for so long that even though it was co-ed by the time I was there prom wasn't a big deal, just another dance. I had friends who were girls but no girlfriend, and it was such a fancy undertaking that I didn't have the energy."

Liam turned to Aidan. "What about you?"

"I was like Edwin. Friends who were girls but no girlfriend. I knew I was more interested in boys than girls, and the whole undertaking was so, I don't know, straight, that I didn't even know how to approach it."

Then they passed a diner where Liam ate with his high school friends, and the orthodontist who'd given Edwin his braces, and soon they were exiting the parkway at Vauxhall

Road in Millburn. From there Aidan followed the phone's directions until they pulled into the driveway of a massive brick mansion. "This is where your cousin lives?" Liam asked Edwin.

"Her husband was a Wall Street guy," he said. "Left her a ton of money."

"Do me a favor, back down the driveway and pull in next door," Edwin said. "These houses are so far apart you could be walking to Newark."

Aidan did as he asked, and he and Liam waited in the car as Edwin walked up to the front door. "You think one of us should have gone with him?" Aidan asked.

"He's safe enough here," Liam said. "Unless cousin Mary Elizabeth has connections with Iranian terrorists."

"You never know," Aidan said.

They watched Edwin ring the bell and speak to the woman who answered. He waited on the stoop for her to bring him a key ring, and then waved goodbye to her.

It was already late afternoon by then, so before they went into the house Aidan followed Edwin's directions to a Trader Joe's on Millburn Avenue. "Ooh, I've missed this store," Aidan said.

"Trust my husband to get excited by a grocery," Liam said, as they walked in.

Aidan got a wagon and moved quickly through the store, adding produce, meats and baked goods. "We don't know how long we're staying, Aidan," Liam said. "You don't need to buy out the whole store."

"Whatever we don't use we'll leave for Mary Elizabeth," Edwin said. "You go to town. It's giving me pleasure to watch you shop, and I'm not getting a lot of that these days."

Liam had blocked Serrano's number after the third call, but before they left the grocery he went outside to call the man. When they were back in the car he recapped.

The Designer of His Own Fortune

"The two men who came at me and Grant are both Iranian citizens who are active in the IDF. Both of them died at the scene, but not before Serrano spoke to one of them, the leader of the group. They wanted the information in the folder, and that they believed I was you. He also said Darius was killed with an AR-15, the same kind the men were using. He's hoping for a ballistics match to the gun used to kill Darius

From the back seat, Edwin gulped. "I'm glad they're dead."

"Serrano expects the IDF to fall apart quickly, after this spectacular failure. Which leaves us with Harvey Grant."

"I don't trust going back to Grant," Aidan said, as he pulled up at a traffic light. "Look what happened this morning."

"I agree," Liam said. "But I don't see any other way forward."

The light turned green and Aidan began moving again. "I have an idea," he said. "Parviz Esfahani."

Liam turned to him. "The kid Darius was mentoring?"

"Who says he has a blog with five thousand viewers. And connections to people in government."

"What can he do for us?" Edwin asked.

"He can release the material from the dossier to the public," Aidan said, as he signaled a turn onto Mary Elizabeth's street. "Removing its value to anyone else."

Chapter 28

Blogger

Liam

They pulled up in the long driveway of Mary Elizabeth's house, and out of habit, Liam looked around. The broad lawn stretched to the street, and the shrubs were too low for anyone to hide behind. He turned to Aidan. "Before we release anything, I want to talk to Louis about what we can and can't give out."

He hopped out of the SUV and went inside, leaving Aidan and Edwin to bring in the groceries. He gathered his cell phone, laptop, the dossier, and the jump drive and carried them into the office Mary Elizabeth's husband had used. They'd already verified that the contents matched, so all he had to do was figure out what to remove from both places.

"Serrano is not happy with you," Louis said, as soon as he answered his phone.

"I'm not particularly thrilled with him. Did he tell you what happened?"

"That you ran away in the middle of the handoff."

"Oh, so he didn't tell you about the two Iranian thugs with AR-15s?"

"He left that part out."

Liam explained what had happened that morning. "Does that mean you still have the dossier and the drive?" Louis asked.

"That's exactly what it means. Aidan has an idea about releasing the information." He explained about Esfahani. "What do you think about that?"

"It makes sense. If the information is no longer secret, then Grant no longer has a reason to protect it. Did Ashoori leave anything to the Organization for a Free Persia in his will?"

"According to a hand-written codicil, witnessed by two hotel employees in DC, they get the remainder of the money in the Cayman account. Grant must know about it. You think that gives him a motive to kill Edwin? To ensure the group gets the money? Edwin could always dispute that codicil, try and prove Grant forced Darius to write it."

"That's a possibility. But according to Serrano, Grant is already in hot water with the State Department. He may need to focus on distancing himself from Darius and the contents of that folder. If you make the contents public, that might actually be good for Grant."

"I can't help that. This information needs to be public. But first I want to go over with you what we have. I don't want to release anything that's going to compromise the personal security of an agent or an ally. Have you had a chance to look at the material we sent you?"

"I did, and I agree with you, we need to release it. Let's start with the photographs. Those can and should all be released. I already flagged anything that had a personal name attached and I used my limited government access to identify anyone who's a US employee. I'll send you the names of all those. They should be redacted."

"I can get Aidan to do that. Upload that list to the archive site and I'll let him know to expect it."

While Louis put the phone down to upload the file, Liam used the time to call out the door to Aidan with instructions on what to do with the file Louis was sending.

"I put all our laundry in the wash so we'll have clean clothes," Adian called back. "I'll get on that next."

"I'm back," Louis said. "File uploaded. Then we come to people on the ground in Iran. I identified a couple of documents you should remove from the archive because they may contain the names of anti-government activists. That leaves us with a bunch of government documents and transcripts of emails and phone conversations."

"Let's go through them."

It took most of an hour to glance through each document and determine if it could be released. Most of the material they had was clearly classified, yet didn't incriminate anyone other than Iranian state actors. All of that stayed in place.

By the time they finished Liam's eyes were tired from staring at the screen, and the rest of his body reminded him that he wasn't as young as he'd been the last time he had to outrun an AR-15, as well as the time in Luxembourg when he'd been shot and ended up in the hospital.

"When are you going to contact this guy?" Louis asked.

"As soon as Aidan finishes what you asked."

"Good luck. Let me know if you need anything more."

Liam hung up, but plans to contact Parviz Esfahani were sidetracked by the smell of dinner cooking in the kitchen. "I'm broiling lamb chops," Aidan said, when Liam walked in. "Salad, baked potatoes and creamed spinach all on the table. I'll have the meat there in a minute."

"What about the photographs? Did you see what Louis uploaded?"

"I did. It was pretty quick to go through and put black boxes over the faces and bodies of the people Louis says we should protect."

"Is that enough?"

"It's not perfect. But I did some cropping and resizing and renaming. The pixels that were used to create those people are long gone."

Liam's stomach grumbled. They hadn't eaten anything since breakfast, so it was probably better to approach Esfahani on a full stomach. Plus he knew nothing of the man's life, so they might not even be able to reach him that evening.

"I haven't eaten this many home-cooked meals in a year," Edwin said as they sat down. "Darius relied on the three Ds—delivery, drive-through and dine out. I kept wanting to take cooking courses at the Sur la Table store in Boca, but he had a finicky palate and never seemed to like anything I made, no matter how hard I worked at it."

"Well, you have a chance to start over," Aidan said.

"Who am I going to cook for?"

"You have friends," Aidan said. "I saw them turn out at the funeral, and from the way they spoke I know they were there for you as much as for Darius. Take a class and then invite some friends over to sample what you've learned."

"I suppose that's a start."

They ate. "These lamb chops are delicious," Edwin said. "So tender and flavorful."

"Organic meat from Trader Joe's," Aidan said. "And I tend to take a light touch when it comes to cooking. When I lived with Blake—that's the guy I was with before Liam – he liked to entertain clients at home, so I took a lot of different cooking classes. I can whip up a Moroccan tagine, Yorkshire pudding, chateaubriand, and a delicious Viennese Linzer torte, among other things. Though I wouldn't serve them all at the same meal."

"You picked a prince," Edwin said to Liam.

"And I treat him like one," Liam said with a smile.

"I can see that." He finished the lamb on his plate and then asked, "How much longer do you think it will be before I'm free?"

"We need to call Parviz Esfahani after dinner and see if he's willing to go along with our plan," Liam said. "After that? Depends on his reach as a blogger, and if news organizations pick up the story."

"The good news is that if he has the right connections, material like this is going to spread fast," Aidan said. "By the weekend we'll be able to judge the fallout. With luck, Harvey Grant is going to be in a lot of hot water, which shifts the pressure off you."

"From your mouth to God's ears," Edwin said.

Liam stared at him. "My mother used to say that all the time."

"I heard that from my father. The two of them grew up together, remember. That's the reason that I keep in touch with Aunt Doris. She reminds me of my father in many ways. Not that he was prejudiced or small-minded. He had a greater exposure to the world and he didn't have the financial pressure that kept her down. But I hear her say things and it's like my father is in the room."

They were quiet for a moment or two, and Liam thought about what Edwin said. Could there be a kinder Doris McCullough inside the shell that presented as his mother? He wasn't convinced.

"Are you going to see her?" Edwin asked.

"Let's get your problems solved first," Liam said. "We don't know how long we'll be able to stay underground here. I'm sure Serrano has ways to track us down, and probably Grant does too."

Aidan stood and began to clear the table. "Then we should call Esfahani as soon as possible."

Aidan rinsed the dishes and Edwin loaded the dishwasher while Liam took one final look at the materials he wanted to send. Then he set his phone in the middle of the kitchen table and called Esfahani's number on speaker.

The voice on the other end was hesitant. "Hello?"

"Parviz, it's Liam McCullough. We have some material you might find interesting for your blog."

He explained what they had.

"This is going to catch fire," Parviz said. "Are you ready for that?"

"We want Edwin and Darius kept out of this," Liam said. "Can you do that? Anonymous source?"

"If that's what you want. When can I see the documents?"

Liam gave him the address for the secure server and the password he'd established for Louis.

"Can you stay on the line while I make sure I can get in?"

"Absolutely. Take a couple of minutes. We'll be here."

In the background they heard Esfahani's fingers on his keyboard. "I'm in," he said. "Downloading now."

"The pictures are going to take extra time to download because they're high-res," Liam said. "If you have any print media interested, they'll want those. Look at the documents first."

"OK."

Again they heard keyboard sounds. "*Siktir!*" he said.

Edwin laughed. "One of Darius's favorite Farsi curses," he said. "According to Darius it's like holy cow."

"A bit dirtier than that," Esfahani said. "You didn't exaggerate when you described these documents."

"Do you think you can get mainstream media attention?" Aidan asked. "The quicker we get this material out to the public, the sooner we remove the threat to Edwin."

"My best posts go out late in the evening," Parviz said. "I'm going to get right on this. The notifications should be in the in-boxes of some very powerful people first thing tomorrow morning. It's going to be a hell of a Thursday for some of them."

"We'll let you get to it," Liam said. "Send us the link as soon as you have it. We have a few useful folks in our own network."

Esfahani ended the call.

"I bought a tarte tatin from Trader Joe's for dessert," Aidan said. "French vanilla ice cream, too. Who's in?"

Liam sat back in his chair as Aidan brought out the pie and ice cream. It was nice to have this peaceful moment, the three of them. Things were going to explode the next day, and they had to recharge in order to be ready.

Chapter 29

Positive Change
Aidan

After Aidan had cleared the dessert dishes, Edwin went to his room and Aidan joined Liam in the living room. "I hope Esfahani is as good as his word," Liam said.

"I do, too. But I read through his blog yesterday and this morning, and he's dropped some big stories in the past. I also did a search for his name and found that he's been quoted often in mainstream media."

The link came through in Liam's email as they were getting ready for bed, and they opened it on their individual laptops. Aidan finished reading first. "He's good," he said. "He tied together a lot of those documents and connected them to incidents already reported in the media."

"I agree. And I appreciate how he tried to tell two sides of the same story, using history. The shah wasn't all bad, and neither are the mullahs. He gave some texture to the story."

"This would be a great basis for a dissertation, if that's what he's aiming for," Aidan said. "Excellent first-hand source material."

"I hate to think of Darius dying for someone's Ph.D."

"The better way to look at it is that Darius's death could result in positive change in the world," Aidan said. "And that's something admirable."

True to his word, by the time they woke on Thursday morning Parviz's blog had made the news. They sat up in bed and checked the news from their respective devices. "I've got the *Washington Post*," Aidan said. "Great headline. 'New Information in the Struggle for Iranian Self-Determination.'"

"The *New York Times* has a similar one." Liam lowered his reading glasses to look over at Aidan's pad. "The *Times* has the story farther down but still on the front page."

They both read in silence until Aidan said, "The *Post* must have known some of this material already. This article is too polished to have been written overnight, and has too many sources and quotes outside of what Parviz published."

"Same with the *Times*," Liam said. "Let's see who else is covering this."

They spent another half-hour combing the Internet. Aidan had learned that because many of his ESL students came from countries where media access was heavily regulated, he had to give them lessons on information literacy as well. He used right-wing, left-wing and relatively unbiased sites like the *Times* and the *Post*, comparing the language used in each.

He had trained them to look for phrases like "some people," because if the author knew the people she was writing about, she should quote them. Similarly "reports say" and "research shows" needed to be backed up with evidence.

For a moment he missed teaching. The reports on Esfahani's revelations would have been a great educational moment, helping his students sort through what was truth and what was opinion, and what was simply evasion.

Aidan's stomach grumbled. "I should get up and make breakfast," he said. "You going to call Serrano?"

"After we eat," Liam said.

They showered and dressed quickly, and Aidan was surprised to find Edwin in the kitchen, making them breakfast. "I remembered that the last time I stayed with her, Mary Elizabeth made waffles, and I haven't had them since. I hope that's okay."

"Any time someone cooks for me is okay," Aidan said. "I'll set the table."

Edwin had found a box of protein-packed mix in his cousin's cabinet, and the result was a nutty, wholesome set of waffles made even better with grade A maple syrup from an artisan farm in Vermont.

After they finished eating and cleared the table, Liam unblocked Serrano's phone number and put his phone in the center of the table. He turned on the speaker so Aidan and Edwin could hear.

"Good morning, Joel," Liam said. "I have Aidan and Edwin on speaker with me. I assume you've read the morning papers."

"I can't say I appreciate the end run you did, but I understand why in the circumstances," Serrano said.

"It was what we had to do to protect Edwin. Do you think he's safe now?"

"We're opening an investigation into Harvey Grant and his connections to those documents," Serrano said. "He certainly had access to some of them during his time at State. It's unclear if he was the one who released them to Mr. Ashoori."

"So he's got bigger problems than coming after Edwin for reprisal or revenge," Aidan said.

"Don't discount him completely. He's a powerful guy, and I believe we're going to learn how powerful over the next few days."

When the call was over, Edwin turned to Liam and Aidan. "When do you think I can go back to Boca?"

"We need to give Serrano a day or two to assemble his case against Grant, and make sure Grant has other things to focus on," Liam said. "And I'd also like to see the fallout from Parviz's blog."

Edwin nodded. "Then we have plenty of time to visit Aunt Doris."

"Only Aidan and I are authorized to drive the rental car," Liam said. "But he can drive you there."

Edwin shook his head. "I want you both to come with me."

Liam stared at his cousin. "I don't know about that, Edwin," Liam said.

"I do. She's your mother, and you need to make things right with her. She won't be around much longer."

"Your mouth to God's ears," Liam said.

"Liam!" Aidan said.

He turned on his husband. "What?"

"She's a flawed person. She said and did hurtful things to you when you were growing up, and she didn't protect you from Big Bill. But that's not a reason to wish her dead."

"It's an expression," Liam said, but he knew that was a lame defense.

"Liam and I will talk about this," Aidan said to Edwin. He tugged on his husband's arm. "Come with me."

They went into the office, and Liam immediately

walked over to the wall of windows that looked out on the yard. Aidan joined him there.

Leaves had fallen during the night and several of the trees were bare. Winter was coming. Without looking at Aidan, Liam said, "I don't know why you're pushing this reunion. You don't like my mother either. The last time you saw her you told her off."

"I know, and I feel bad about that. It was a primal urge to defend you, and I'm sorry if I hurt her." He took a deep breath. "I know you didn't have the relationship with your parents that I had with mine. I had some issues with them, but now that they're both gone I can't do anything to make things better, for me or for them. You still have that chance."

Aidan put his arm around his husband's waist. "Plus there's something we've learned about your cousin. The brightly colored clothes, the fancy watch and the jeweled rings are a front he puts up to the world. He is as tenacious as a pit bull when he wants to be. He's not going to let up."

Liam crossed his arms over his chest. "And you think I won't be able to stand up to him?"

Aidan smiled. "I have many years of experience watching you make difficult decisions. I know that you resist at first, but then you think through the whole scenario and come out the right side."

"You think seeing my mother while we're here is the right side?"

"I do. But I also know that I can't push you. You have to make the decision yourself."

Aidan left Liam in the office and returned to the living room, where he picked up his laptop and began looking for additional follow-up to the revelations Parvis Esfahani had posted. He found an interview Parviz had given to another blogger. As promised he did not reveal that Darius was the source of the information. However, the blogger was persistent, and dug around in Parviz's earlier posts, a few of which mentioned Darius.

The blogger rehashed Darius's murder, and speculated that he might have been involved. "That isn't good." Aidan went looking for Liam, whom he found on the exercise bike in the study. His head was down and he was pedaling madly.

"Liam?"

His husband looked up, still pedaling.

"Sorry to disturb you but you need to look at this."

Liam switched into cool-down mode on the bike, continuing to pedal slowly. "What is it?"

"A blogger is connecting the dots between Darius's death and the release of the stuff from the folder and the jump drive."

Liam blew out a deep breath. "How bad is it?"

"Not bad yet. Just speculation. And it's only one guy, so far as I can see."

Liam dismounted the bike and took the laptop from Aidan. He read through the blog post quickly. "What do you think? Do we ask Parviz to issue a denial?"

"My instinct is to ignore it," Aidan said. "Darius is only a bit player in this particular drama. With luck it'll fall between the cracks. After all, Parviz is only able to connect the material to us and to Edwin. He doesn't know where Darius got it."

"Neither do we." Liam wiped his forehead with a towel. "I'm not feeling this bike. I think I'll go for a run. My head is still muddled."

"I'll be here with Edwin," Aidan said. "And hope that nothing else happens."

Chapter 30

Can of Worms

Liam

Liam was glad that Aidan had anticipated the cooler weather and packed sweatpants and a long-sleeved T-shirt for him. He dressed, stretched, and then loped down Mary Elizabeth's long driveway to the street.

Though it wasn't a gated community, the neighborhood was well-manicured and the sidewalks were broad. The houses were all set well back from the street, with still-green lawns scattered with fallen leaves. A world away from the neighborhood of close-packed houses where he'd grown up, where only a porch and a short set of steps separated the house from the broken sidewalk. Neighbors could see into your windows, and he was sure everyone knew when Big Bill had had too much to drink and yelled and struck out at whoever was around.

They hadn't been poor, exactly, he thought as he ran. Lower middle class, probably. Big Bill worked often enough to pay the mortgage. Most of the people around them were in similar circumstances, first-generation American parents without much education, struggling to make things better for their kids.

A police cruiser passed him, going slowly, and he waved. Though it was a rich area, there had to be people who jogged, and his regular pace indicated he was exercising rather than casing homes or running away from something.

Although that's what he was doing, he thought, as he turned right, hoping to make a big circuit that would take him back to Mary Elizabeth's. He was running away from his background, his family, all the pain he had tried to leave behind when he left New Brunswick for Naval Station Great Lakes, on the shore of Lake Michigan.

It was the perfect place for him at the time. He learned to channel his energy and his anger, to challenge his body and his mind. He excelled at every challenge, and he quickly realized that Boot Camp was a lot like college, only with more direction and rigor.

His drill sergeant recognized something in him and recommended that he take the advanced workout program to prepare for the BUDs training, to become a SEAL. It was the first time someone had actively mentored him, and it changed the direction of his life.

He turned another corner, starting to feel the burn in his legs and chest. Passing the BUDs course was the first time he felt proud and confident, and the other members of his team became like the brothers he'd never had. He'd worked his ass off, seen the world, and faced down dangers most men never had to.

But at the same time he was fighting against his attraction to men. The ban against openly homosexual individuals serving in the armed forces was fully in place, and gradually he couldn't see a way forward. Then after a particularly brutal battle he realized that he had risked his life because it meant so little to him.

He came out to his commanding officer, even though he knew it meant the end of his naval career. He'd gone back to New Brunswick for a short time. Big Bill was dead by then, but Doris only saw him as a failure, and he knew he couldn't stay. An old friend recommended him for a bodyguard stint in Tunis, and he grabbed the opportunity like a lifeline.

Once he was there, he realized he could use the same skills he'd developed in the Navy in private life, and then he'd met Aidan, and things had never been bad again.

Sure, there had been tough times. He rounded another corner for the final stretch back to Mary Elizabeth's house. He and Aidan had fought and made up, disagreed on strategy, had good sex and boring sex, made friends and a home together.

He couldn't explain all that to his mother, though. They spoke erratically on the phone, and she generally ignored the fact that Aidan was there in the background. She'd disapproved of him the one time they met, ten years before.

He'd never told her about their marriage. He was sure she'd have caustic remarks. And yet, she had accepted Edwin and Darius. Was it because Edwin sent her money? Or had her attitude really softened over the years?

By the time he returned to the house, he still hadn't decided. Should he see his mother or not? Was he a coward for refusing to face her, or pragmatic?

Aidan and Edwin ordered take-out from a burger place Edwin remembered, and the three of them sat around the kitchen table eating. It had been a long time since Liam ate a good American cheeseburger, and he savored every bite.

"I keep remembering an old Persian proverb Darius used to say," Edwin said. "Every man is the designer of his own fortune." He picked up a French fry and dipped it in ketchup, then ate it. "He used it to be a definition of entrepreneurship. That he was the one responsible for making a successful business."

"Sounds reasonable," Liam said.

"But now I'm thinking about it differently," Edwin said. "That Darius caused all this trouble. If he hadn't been so obsessed with Persia and going back there, then he'd still be alive today." He waved his hand. "This is all his fault."

"I worked with a lot of immigrants back when I was a teacher," Aidan said. "And many of them were sad to have left their homes, particularly those who had been chased away. But I don't think you can put all the blame on Darius."

"Who then?" Edwin asked. "Harvey Grant? The mullahs? All these crazy political groups?"

"All of the above," Liam said. "One thing that we've learned in our years in personal protection is that there's no one cause for the evil in the world. Some people make poor choices which bring them into conflict with bad actors. Flaunting wealth in a poor area, for example. Or making investments in businesses they know are fraudulent, or controlled by criminals."

"Sometimes people who speak out for what they believe in are targeted," Aidan added. "We've had a number of cases like that. And for some, it's a case of being in the wrong place at the wrong time."

"The point is, you can't blame Darius for everything," Liam said. "He certainly played a part in what happened, but Grant took advantage of him, and that put a target on his back."

Edwin shook his head. "I understand all that. But it's easier right now to blame Darius. For getting involved in this, for dying, for leaving me."

Liam looked at Aidan. He hoped they would never come to this point, where one bad decision could separate them. He reached out and took his husband's hand and squeezed, and Aidan squeezed back.

They said goodnight to Edwin soon after that, and they retired to their room. Liam played a military simulation game on his laptop for a couple of hours as Aidan read. By the time the game ended, Aidan was already asleep. Liam stripped down and then slid into bed beside his husband. This was where he was happiest, with this man beside him. He could face whatever the future held as long as they were together. He refused to make a comparison to Edwin and Darius. He and Aidan had no secrets from each other, and they always had each other's back.

He slept deeply, and when he awoke and turned to reach for Aidan on Friday morning, the other side of the bed was empty. Not the best way to wake up, he thought.

He pulled on shorts and a T-shirt and went downstairs, where Aidan and Edwin were sharing coffee and Danish pastry in the kitchen.

"Our story is getting bigger," Aidan said, passing him an iPad open to the *New York Times*. "The House Foreign Affairs Committee is calling for an investigation into government support of both the regime in Iran and the competing groups. Grant is mentioned by name, but he hasn't been arrested for anything yet."

Liam took the iPad and read the report, then surfed around for more news as Aidan handed him a coffee and a pastry.

"I spoke to Aunt Doris this morning," Edwin said. "I'm going over there this afternoon. Aidan has offered to drop me off there and pick me up when I'm ready to leave."

"He won't need to do that," Liam said, surprising himself. "I'm going with you."

"What changed your mind?" Edwin asked.

Liam looked at him. Both he and Aidan were waiting to hear. "I can't say exactly," he admitted. "It's a whole bunch of things."

"Well, whatever they are, I'm glad you're doing this," Edwin said. "Aunt Doris will be very happy."

"We'll see how happy she is later," Liam grumbled, then bit into the flaky pastry. When he joined Aidan in their room after breakfast, his husband was fussing over clothes he'd laid out on the bed.

"We're wearing Agence polo shirts and khakis this afternoon," Aidan said. "I'm afraid that's all I brought. The rest of our clothes are still at Edwin's in Boca."

"I don't want to make a big deal of this," Liam said. "We go over there, we say hello, I ask about my sisters and their families, and we leave."

"If you say so," Aidan said.

"I still have a bad feeling about this. It is Friday the 13th, after all."

"We'll drive carefully."

"And travel armed," Liam said.

Aidan didn't argue, which was a good thing. Liam was focusing all his energy on getting through the visit to his mother, and he didn't need arguments on top of it.

They spent the morning reviewing more news reports of the revealed documents. Liam spoke briefly to Joel Serrano and to Louis Fleck, and then after lunch they got into the SUV.

Aidan drove, with Edwin riding shotgun and giving Aidan directions. Liam didn't recognize much—it had been ten years since his last visit, and another dozen since he'd driven these streets regularly. Familiar stores were shuttered and some streets looked desolate, while other areas were booming with new high-rises and shopping centers. Rutgers continued its inexorable progress toward taking over every available piece of land near the campus.

He recognized the house, though. It needed a coat of paint, and the climbing roses Doris had tried to cultivate along the porch railing were dead. They pulled up on the street and Aidan parked. Edwin hopped out, and Aidan turned to Liam from the front seat. "We can still drop him here and get a coffee," he said.

"No, I should see her." Liam got out of the SUV and sniffed the air. It smelled the same—a combination of automobile exhaust and fertilizer, though he couldn't imagine anyone in the neighborhood taking such good care of their patches of grass.

Edwin was already on the porch, like an eager golden retriever. He rang the bell as Aidan and Liam came up behind him.

Doris had gotten old, Liam thought. That was the problem with only speaking to someone on the phone for ten years—you spotted the changes immediately. She was thinner than she had been, and her blue polka-dot dress, which had once fit her very well, now hung awkwardly from her shoulders.

"You look lovely as usual, Aunt Doris," Edwin said, and kissed her cheek.

But she wasn't paying attention to her nephew. Her eyes were on her sonny boy. Liam stepped up beside his cousin. "Hi, Mom."

"So you're back," she said. "I didn't believe it when Eddie said he was bringing you over."

"I'm here. In the flesh."

He turned at the sound of screeching brakes on the street behind him, and to his horror he saw the stock of an AR-15 stuck out the passenger window. "Everybody get down!" he yelled, as he pushed Edwin into Doris.

By the time he turned, Aidan had drawn the Glock Gardner had given him and begun firing. Liam body-blocked his mother and his cousin and pulled his own gun.

Aidan was down on one knee, firing in through the open window of the car, a late model Toyota. Liam couldn't get an angle through the window, so he focused on shooting out the tires. With luck, Aidan would incapacitate the shooter and the driver would be forced to abandon the vehicle, giving them a shot at him.

But instead, the car horn began to blare, and the AR-15 fell to the street. Then the car began to move erratically forward, veering to the right until it smashed into a parked pickup truck.

Aidan scrambled up the sidewalk to the porch. "Everyone okay?" he asked.

"What in the name of Jesus, Mary, and Joseph?" Doris said.

Liam turned back to his mother. She was sprawled on the floor of her house, Edwin crouched beside her. The hem of her polka-dot dress had risen up, exposing her skinny calves.

"My fault," Edwin said. "I think those men were aiming for me."

Liam pulled his phone out of his pocket and dialed 911. He gave the operator the address and requested police. She asked him to stay on the line, but he hung up.

"The cops are going to confiscate these guns," he said. "And trace them back to the CIA. Which is going to open a whole can of worms."

"Can't be helped," Aidan said. "Now let's get everyone inside."

Chapter 31

Bad Omen

Liam

Liam helped his mother up and dusted off her dress. "You're sure you're OK?" he asked.

She felt her sides. "Didn't break a hip," she said. "That's a good day." She turned to her son. "You going to tell me what's going on?"

Liam turned to Aidan. "Will you stay out here and wait for the cops?"

"Sure. Take my gun, though."

He handed it to Liam, who grabbed the warm barrel. "Edwin, get my mom settled, please," he said. "I need to deal with these."

Aidan had pumped ten of the seventeen bullets in the cartridge into the Toyota. Liam emptied the rest of the bullets, then did the same for his own gun. He'd only gotten off two shots, and he had to remind himself that Aidan was not only the better shot, but had a better position.

He laid the guns on the top of the stand that held a statue of Jesus. "Keep an eye on these for me, will you?" he murmured to the statue.

Then he turned to his mother and his cousin. Edwin had begun explaining what Darius had done, and how his lies had resulted in so much danger.

"That's all right," Doris said, patting his hand. "I know what it's like to have a man give you trouble."

She looked up at Liam. "You and your friend taking care of Eddie?"

"My husband," Liam said. "Aidan's my husband."

"You never said," Doris said. "I would have sent you a gift."

Liam wanted to laugh, but he resisted the urge. "We've been helping Edwin get out of this trouble." He sat down across from her. "How have you been, Mom? You're losing weight."

"My doctor has me on these pills to reduce my craving for cigarettes, and turns out they shut down my appetite, too."

"You stopped smoking?" Liam asked. "I thought you never would."

"Give the house a sniff," she said. "You smell any smoke?"

He did as he was told. For as long as he could remember, tobacco smoke from both his parents had ingrained itself into the walls and the furniture. But now, he could barely smell it. "Good for you," he said.

"It was Andrea guilted me into it," she said. "She studied biology in school and came over with all these pictures of how bad your lungs get after smoking. She said she wanted me to be a great-grandmother."

She looked at Liam. "Not going to get there from you and Aidan."

He was stunned that his mother remembered Aidan's

name. She never asked about him when they spoke, though Liam made sure to drop his name into conversation.

"No, you're not," Liam said. "But you've got Andrea and Tommy. How's Tommy doing?"

They lapsed into the usual conversation they had on the phone. Out of the corner of his eye Liam saw flashing red and blue lights on the street and knew it would only be a matter of time before the cops were at the door.

But he focused on his mother. It was sweet, having a three-way conversation with Doris and Edwin, as Edwin brought up memories that Liam had forgotten. A time when they'd all gone to the Great Adventure theme park, and Jeannie had fallen into a fountain while pretending to be a ballerina.

Then the front door opened and Aidan stepped in. "The police would like to speak with you and Edwin," he said.

The detective was a middle-aged man who looked Pakistani or Indian. "I'm detective Kashani from the Criminal Investigations Department," he said. "I've already met Mr. Greene and gotten some background from him. I'd like to speak with Mr. McCullough, please."

Liam rose. "We can go in the kitchen," he said. "But first, you'll want to take possession of our weapons. Over there on the table."

"Thank you." Kashani pulled on a pair of blue gloves and checked first one gun, then the second, and counted the bullets. Then he put everything into a series of evidence bags.

"This is like an episode of *Law and Order*," Doris said.

"We do our best," Kashani said. Then Liam led him to the kitchen.

They sat at the scarred linoleum table. "Mr. Greene has

laid out a very interesting story," the detective said. "I'd like to hear your perspective, please." He put his phone on the table between them. "And I'd like to record this, if you don't mind."

Liam went back to the beginning, to Edwin's first phone call. Then he laid everything out step by step, leading to their run from DC and hiding out at Mary Elizabeth's house in Short Hills.

"You didn't notice anyone watching the house there?" Kashani asked. "Or following you here?"

Liam shook his head. "Honestly, we thought we were done, once we released that information to the media. And I haven't seen my mother in ten years, so I was focused on getting here and what kind of conversation we'd have."

Kashani asked a few more questions, then shut off the recording. "Now, if you'd have your cousin come in here, please."

"Certainly." Liam rose and pulled out his wallet. "This is Joel Serrano's card, with his cell number on the back. He'll confirm that he had another officer get us those Glocks."

Kashani took the card. "Thank you."

Liam sent Edwin into the kitchen and sat back down across from his mother. "Your husband and I have been getting acquainted," his mother said. "Such a shame he doesn't have people here anymore."

He stared at his mother. It was like a different person had inhabited her body. She was being nice, a side of her he'd rarely seen growing up. Usually reserved for people from Our Lady of Perpetual Help.

"Doris didn't tell you about her cancer scare, because she didn't want to worry you," Aidan said.

"You had cancer?" Liam couldn't help the accusing tone

in his voice, like he was complaining about a criminal record.

"It wasn't nothing," Doris said. "A lump in my breast. They took it out. Early-stage cancer, they said. I had a few radiation treatments which made me sicker than a dog, so I gave up on them. Been back for checkups every year, March 25. I know the date because it's the Solemnity of the Annunciation of the Lord."

She turned to Aidan. "That's nine months before the birth of Christ," she said. "I always liked that holiday because I knew exactly when I got pregnant with Billy."

Oh, God, not that story again, Liam thought, but Doris had already launched into it. She and Big Bill had gone to the Jersey shore for their honeymoon, and they did it three times that first night. By the next morning she knew she was pregnant, and sure enough, nine months later there was her sonny boy.

"And they called him Big Bill for a reason," Doris added. "Not just because of his height, if you know what I mean."

He glared at Aidan, daring him to say anything about his own size, but Aidan was smart enough to keep his mouth shut.

Edwin returned to join them, but Kashani remained in the kitchen for a few minutes. When he came out, as Liam expected, he had confirmed their story with Joel Serrano.

"Mr. Gallagher gave me the address where you're staying in Short Hills," he said. "I'd appreciate it if you didn't leave for a few days. Give us a chance to wrap everything up here."

"What happened to the men in the car?" Liam asked. "Were they both shot?"

"Your husband is quite the marksman," Kashani said. "Preliminary look indicates he hit the man with the gun three times. One of those bullets went through him and into the driver, who collapsed against the steering wheel and triggered the airbag."

"Are they still alive?" Liam asked.

Kashani nodded. "Ambulance took them both to the hospital. We won't know their condition for a while, though."

He nodded toward the door. "Well, then, I'll let you continue your visit. But I'd like all three of you to come to the main station on Kirkpatrick Street tomorrow for formal statements."

After he was gone, Liam looked at Aidan. "I told you Friday the 13th was a bad omen."

"And the day isn't finished yet," Aidan said.

"I want to make a call." Liam rose and went into the kitchen, where he dialed Serrano's number.

"You're still getting in trouble," Serrano said. "I told you the safest place was to stay where we could keep an eye on you."

"We're managing on our own. Any idea who those shooters were?"

"It took some persuading, but the detective finally passed on the identification they were carrying. Both of them are Irani nationals. They belong to a faction that is backed by the politicians rather than the mullahs. Our best guess right now is that like IDF, they wanted to kill Mr. Gallagher to shut off any future funds to the group his husband was supporting."

"Jesus, these people keep coming out of the woodwork. Anybody else we should watch out for?"

"At this point I think Mr. Gallagher is safe, though I suggest he gives an interview to Parviz Esfahani and states that he has no involvement with any of the groups and no intention to continue funding any of them."

"You think that will matter?"

"It can't hurt. A lot of what's going on now is above my pay grade, but the documents Mr. Ashoori had in his possession implicate a wide range of individuals and groups. My guess is that they're all going to be scrambling to reorganize, and they'll be too busy saving their own hides to come after Mr. Gallagher."

"You might have said that this morning," Liam said. "But things have changed."

"I never promised to be an all-seeing oracle," Serrano said. "Keep your eyes open. And you didn't hear this from me, but if you feel the need to stay armed, go across the border to Pennsylvania. Jersey requires a permit from local law enforcement to buy a weapon, but in the Keystone State there's no waiting period. No license or permit to purchase required, and there's no training required."

"Makes me glad to be a Jersey boy," Liam said. "But I'll keep that information under advisement."

Before he went back to the living room, he looked at the map on his phone and established that the easiest way to get to Pennsylvania was to take I-287 to I-78 and cross the Delaware to Easton. There were several gun shops there—but all of them closed at five that day.

He went back to the living room. "We've got to get moving," he said. "We'll come back tomorrow after we talk to the police, Mom."

"I'm sure Franny and Jeannie would like to see you," she said. "Andrea and Tommy too."

"We'll make it a family reunion," Edwin said. "I'll call

you tomorrow and we'll pick up some food on our way here."

Edwin kissed Doris on the cheek, and so did Liam. Aidan tried to shake her hand, but she pulled him in for a kiss, too. "Son-in-law," she said. "I haven't had one of those in a while. Hopefully you'll last longer than the other ones."

Chapter 32

Gun Shop
Aidan

Aidan got into the driver's seat, and Edwin sat beside him, with Liam in the rear. "Can you get us to I-287, Edwin?" Liam asked. "Or should I pull up directions on the phone?"

"Which way are we going? East or west?"

"West. We're heading to Pennsylvania."

"Then I can get you there."

He directed them past St. Peter's Hospital on Easton Avenue. "I was born there," Liam said as they approached it. "Franny and Jeannie too. That bar over there, McShane's? That was one of Big Bill's hangouts."

Aidan was intrigued by this look into Liam's growing-up years. "Did you always live in the same house?"

"When I was born Doris and Big Bill were living in an apartment a few blocks from here," Liam said. "We moved around a couple of times until they bought the house."

"With money from grandpa," Edwin said.

Liam leaned forward. "Really?"

"Grandma got a payout from his railroad pension when he died, and she split it between your mom and my dad.

Aunt Doris and Uncle Bill bought the house, and my father put his money into IBM stock."

They took the Landing Lane Bridge over the Raritan. "Turn left on Route 18, and it'll run you into 287." Edwin turned back to Liam. "A reason why we're going to Pennsylvania?"

"Gun control laws are non-existent there," Liam said. "And even though Joel Serrano says we're out of danger, I'd prefer to be safe."

Once they got onto the highway, they left the urban sprawl behind, driving through rolling countryside, the verge lined with trees coming into full color. "This is the Jersey I love," Aidan said, as traffic eased and he could put his foot down on the pedal.

"Me too," Edwin said. "People outside the state don't realize this exists. All they know is the factories along the Turnpike, the smell, and the Newark slums."

"Which weren't slums when we were growing up," Liam said. "Big Bill used to have cousins near Weequahic Park, and when we'd go visit them the other kids and I would ride bikes in the park. It seemed so much nicer than New Brunswick."

They drove and drove. Eighteen-wheelers filled with the goods Americans craved. Pickup trucks so tall you needed a stepladder to get into them. And crammed in between, tiny Fiats and Mini Coopers. The vast differences between Americans. He'd forgotten that, living overseas for so long.

"What time do these gun shops close?" Aidan asked as they approached Philipsburg, on the Jersey side of the Delaware."

"Five o'clock," Liam said. "We've still got an hour."

They made quick work at the gun store. Liam knew

exactly what he wanted for both of them, including outside-the-waistband holsters.

"What kind of ammo do you want?" the clerk asked. "Full metal jacket or hollow point?"

Aidan knew Liam preferred hollow point because they expanded on impact, had more stopping power, and were more likely to take down your opponent than FMJ. As expected, Liam asked for hollow points for both guns.

"Can I interest you in Nightsticks for these?" the clerk asked. "The TSM-11G 150-Lumen Rechargeable Tactical Mounted Weapon Light gives you a green laser that's good as daylight."

"We'll take two," Liam said.

Edwin handed over his credit card without complaint.

While Liam finished the transaction, Aidan pulled Edwin aside. "We won't be able to take these back to France with us, but we'll give you some quick lessons before we leave."

"I'd appreciate that. I'm not planning to carry a gun to Whole Foods, but I'd like to have one in the house for protection."

They walked back outside, and Edwin's stomach grumbled. "You think we can get dinner out here?" he asked. "I know a charming waterfront restaurant along the Delaware."

"I think we're fine," Liam said. "I kept an eye out as we were driving and I didn't identify anyone suspicious."

While Aidan followed Edwin's directions, Liam loaded both guns. When they arrived, Liam handed him one of the Glocks, and he slid it into the holster, then untucked his shirt so the tail hung over it.

The hostess led them to a table that faced the water, and

Aidan and Edwin took the river view seats, while, Liam faced the front door.

"This has certainly been an eventful couple of weeks," Edwin said, after they'd placed their order. "I don't know what I'd have done without the two of you."

Aidan shrugged. "Things might have worked out very differently if Harvey Grant approached you directly. You would have found the key to the safe deposit box and handed it over to him, and you'd have been done."

"What about all these other people?" Edwin asked. "The ones who want me to stop the funding that Darius started. I doubt Grant would have protected me from them."

"Woulda, coulda, shoulda," Liam said. "Can't think like that. We face what we have to."

Dinner arrived, and they ate. The dock beside the restaurant was lit with strings of fairy lights and in such nice surroundings it was hard for Aidan to remember what a day they'd had.

When they got back to the SUV, Aidan removed his holster and slid the Glock into the door pocket beside him. Not ideal, since he wasn't a lefty, but he wasn't that worried either. The dinner had lulled them into believing everything was on its way to resolution.

As they began the long drive back to Short Hills, Edwin nodded off in the front seat, and a glance in the rear-view mirror told Aidan that Liam was doing the same thing.

He was glad that Liam was finally willing to engage more with his mother. Doris McCullough was a character, but she seemed to have overcome some of her prejudices. Regardless of how she'd behaved in the past, it was going to be good for Liam to be in closer contact with her.

Which made him think of his own family. While he was

in North Jersey, did he want to see if he could connect with his cousin Ellen? It had been great to talk to her, and she was the closest family he had. If he and Liam and Edwin had to stick around Short Hills for a few days, he wanted to head over to Basking Ridge and see Ellen and her family, if they were available.

When he reached the exit on I-78, he used the time at the traffic light to plug Mary Elizabeth's address into his GPS, and then got directions back to her house. It was after 8:00 by the time he pulled into the driveway. He reached over and removed the Glock from the door pocket. "We're here," he said, and Edwin stirred.

Liam was awake immediately. "Sorry, I should have been more vigilant," he said.

"No one followed us, at least not the last couple of miles through the residential neighborhoods," Aidan said. "And the advantage of this long driveway is that I did some twists and turns to light up the area around the house. Looks clear."

"I'll go first," Liam said.

He stepped out of the SUV as Edwin finally came awake. "Oh, we're at Mary Elizabeth's."

He reached for the door handle, but Aidan reached over to stop him. "Give us a minute to establish safety."

"Still?"

"Can't be too careful."

"But we didn't bother at the restaurant."

"No one followed us to the gun shop, or from there to the restaurant," Aidan said. "We had good visibility. Someone might still be planning to harm you, and have figured out we're staying here."

Liam engaged the Nightstick and surveyed the perimeter, casting a green glow on the lawn and bushes. "Looks clear," he called.

Aidan and Edwin got out, and they all hurried into the house. "How much longer am I going to have to live like this?" Edwin asked.

"Another day or two," Liam said. "And there's probably nothing to worry about. But you're still our client and it's our job to protect you."

"We slipped up when we went to see Liam's mom," Aidan said. "We let our guard down. Fortunately you didn't get hurt, but that was a warning to us."

Edwin nodded. "Well, I'm bushed. I'll see you in the morning."

After checking the doors, windows and alarm system, Aidan and Liam climbed up to the master bedroom and Liam began to strip off his clothes. Aidan said, "What was that quote from Churchill about getting shot?"

Liam paused, his shirt and shoes off, his slacks open. "Nothing in life is so exhilarating as to be shot at without result."

"I could think of something more exhilarating we could do," Aidan said. He'd already shucked his Agence polo shirt and his slacks, and all he wore was a pair of boxer shorts decorated with tiny maps of France.

Liam looked at him and smiled. "Let me guess. You want me to find Banneret on that map."

"Or something else," Aidan said, and he shifted the placket of his shorts so that his erection popped out.

"Oh, you're making that too easy for me." Liam dropped his slacks and peeled off his jockstrap, and joined Aidan in the bed. Maybe something good would come out of Friday the 13th after all.

Chapter 33

No More Secrets

Aidan

Saturday morning, Liam was already up and out running when Aidan awoke. He turned on his side and inhaled the fragrance his husband had left behind. His dick hardened again, but there was no one to take care of it, so he performed his morning ablutions, pulled on a clean pair of slacks and a T-shirt, and went downstairs.

By then, Liam had returned, and he and Edwin were sitting at the kitchen table. "Look who's the sleepyhead this morning," Edwin said. "I'm a light sleeper, and the walls in this house are surprisingly thin."

He grinned at both of them. "I'm glad you two are still so attracted to each other. I miss that."

Aidan turned away so that Edwin wouldn't see him blush. "I'm sure you can find someone else," he said. "You're still young, you're good-looking and you're in shape."

"And you have money," Liam said.

"All of that is relative in Boca Raton," Edwin said. "There are a lot of younger, better-looking men, and a lot who have more money than I do. But I'm ready to be on my own for a while, at least. No more secrets that way. I'm more worried about how what's happened over the last two weeks are ingrained in my head by now. I don't know that I'll ever get over it."

"You will," Liam said. "Aidan and I have seen a lot of clients through traumatic situations. It will take a while, but the short-term memories will disappear, and the long-term ones will get cloudy. You'll probably remember bits and pieces again, and maybe you'll be nervous for a while."

"How do you keep doing this?" Edwin asked. "I hesitate to ask how many people you've killed."

"I don't keep track," Liam said. "But most of our work is not dangerous. We're hired by clients who want to feel secure, and we evaluate any potential threats and watch out for them. Usually having personal protection is enough to scare away trouble."

"Who hires you, then?" Edwin asked.

Aidan took that question. "Rich people. We spend a lot of time ushering women from the Emirates as they go shopping on the Riviera, for example. We have a reputation as a gay couple, so the male clients trust us with their wives and daughters."

"Really? You can be out like that?"

"It's 2023, Edwin," Liam said. "Yes, there are people out there who are prejudiced against gay men. But sometimes we use those prejudices to our advantage."

At eleven o'clock they were at the police station on Kirkpatrick Street, a modern brick and stucco building. They gave their names and Detective Kashani came out to get them. He left Liam and Aidan in a waiting room, and took Edwin into an interview room to get his formal statement.

Liam leaned his head back and stretched out his legs. "This is going to be a while," he said.

"I never understand why we have to give a formal statement after an incident," Aidan said. "Kashani recorded everything we said yesterday."

"And today he'll be looking to trip us up. See if we change anything. Add anything new or leave anything out."

"But we're the victims in this situation."

"That's the way we see it. The police have two men in the hospital who were shot with our guns. They need to make sure all the pieces fit."

Liam closed his eyes and woke again as Edwin arrived with Kashani. "Mr. Greene?" the detective asked, and Aidan went with him.

Kashani led him to a stark interview room with a window to one side. "Have a seat," he said, motioning to a simple wooden chair. Across from him was a laptop with a camera attached to the top. Kashani hit a button on the computer and the camera came to life.

"I am Detective Donald Kashani of the New Brunswick Police Department. This is a non-custodial interview with Mr. Aidan Greene, resident of Banneret-les-Vaux, France, regarding an incident which occurred at approximately 2:45 PM on Friday, October 13, 2023." He added Doris's address.

"This interview will be recorded on a DVR machine for use in any and all prosecutions resulting from the events of that day. Mr. Greene, do you give your consent to this recording?"

"I do," Aidan said.

Kashani stated the date and time of the interview and began his questions. "Please state for the record your employment."

Aidan gave him information on the Agence de Securité including the company address and phone number. "I have my employer's permission to give you a copy of our employment contract with Mr. Edwin McCullough."

He opened the folder he'd brought and handed over the printed page. At Kashani's direction, he explained the kind of work he and Liam did in close protection, and the circumstances which led to Edwin hiring them.

Further questions led to a discussion of the events of the previous two weeks. Since Kashani had already spoken with Joel Serrano, Aidan felt comfortable releasing the agent's name, though he did not mention Will Gardner. He didn't know the address of the safe house in Virginia, nor would he have revealed it without Serrano's permission.

It was a long narrative, and it took a lot of brain power to remember everything. Occasionally Aidan had to stop and back up, explaining, for example, that they had met Mary Elizabeth at Darius's funeral. "I'm afraid I don't know her last name or where she resides in Florida during the winter," he said. "But I can give you the address where we have been staying in Short Hills."

He continued to narrate the story. "Did anyone know you were planning to visit New Brunswick yesterday?" Kashani asked.

"As far I know, only my husband, Mr. Edwin McCullough, and Mrs. Doris McCullough. I don't think Liam or Edwin told anyone. I can't speak for Doris."

"Did you notice anyone following you when you left Short Hills?"

Aidan shook his head. "I was focused on following Edwin's directions. Usually Liam is responsible for watching our backs, but I know he was concerned about seeing his mother again after so many years."

Kashani asked a few more questions about Aidan's marksmanship and his response to the two men with rifles.

"My ability is at least half genetic," he said. "I polished my skills in close protection training, and Liam and I regularly practice threat responses. I didn't think at all, just went into action."

"Very impressive," Kashani said. He turned to the computer. "That concludes my interview."

He hit a button on the laptop and the camera shut down. "I didn't want to say it on camera, but I doubt there are many men on our force who would have the reaction time and the accuracy you did. I'm surprised that you don't have law enforcement experience."

It wasn't until he stood that Aidan realized how much energy the interview had taken from him. He took a couple of deep breaths and followed the detective back into the hallway.

Chapter 34

In the End

Liam

Liam was surprised at how long Aidan was in the interview with Kashani. But then, his partner was good with words and had learned how much detail to provide to support his story.

Liam was interested in all the technology, and knowing how it could be watched over and over again by a wide range of people made him terse. It was almost like being back in the closet, worrying about how much information he could provide without revealing something he preferred to keep secret.

He gave a quick summary of his career, how he had met Aidan, and how they had moved to France to work for the Agence. When it came to how they had come to work for Edwin, he eliminated all the family stuff, and responded to Kashani's questions with short, pithy answers.

"What are your plans now?" Kashani asked as the interview came to its close.

"As soon as we can, we'll escort our client back to his home in Florida. Then Aidan and I will return to France. Do you need us to stay here any longer?"

"These depositions should cover what we need. We have some witness statements from neighbors that support your positions," Kashani said. "All we have against the Iranians here are minor weapons offenses. So hopefully this will be an open-and-shut case. The DA will take a plea bargain and most likely hand the Iranians over to the State Department for deportation. But if this does go to trial, we might have to subpoena you and Mr. Greene to appear."

"We are always willing to assist law enforcement," Liam said.

"That is, when you don't take the law into your own hands," Kashani said tartly. "You're free to go."

When Liam walked out, he found Aidan and Edwin in close conversation. "We're ready to go," he said. "Aidan, see when you can get us reservations back to Florida."

"Already have them," Aidan said. "Tomorrow afternoon, Newark to Fort Lauderdale."

"You can't get us out today?"

"We're going back to Doris's, remember?" Edwin said. "Family party."

Though he wanted to protest, Liam knew it would sound petty, and in the end be useless.

"We already ordered platters of food from European Provisions," Edwin said. "It was my dad's favorite deli. Do you remember us bringing food from there, years ago?"

Liam struggled to remember. That should have been a good time, the rich relatives bringing lunch. But he couldn't.

"As long as you like it," he said.

"Ah, they made the best ham and cheese sandwich ever. They called it the hangover, with Polish ham, smoked ham, salami, gouda cheese and beer mustard." He smiled. "Your mother called it that Polack place and she turned up her nose, but she ate everything in front of her."

"That sounds like Doris," Liam said. "A nasty epithet for every ethnic group. Spics, wops, bluegums."

"Who's a bluegum?" Aidan asked.

"Used to mean an African American with very dark skin, but Doris used it for any Black person she thought was lazy and unwilling to work," Liam said. "At least she never used the N-word. I'll give her that."

They stopped at the deli to pick up the platters Edwin had ordered, and by the time they arrived at Doris's house both his sisters were there, along with his niece and nephew and some other old family friends.

Liam was surprised at how happy everyone seemed to see him, and how good it felt to be seen. He introduced Aidan as his husband and nobody blinked an eye. His nephew Tommy was shy at first, until Liam reminded him of how they'd played ball together in the back yard when Tommy was a boy. "How long ago was that?" Liam asked.

"You haven't been back for ten years," Tommy said. "By the time you come back again you'll be too old to do anything."

"You think?" Liam asked, grabbing him in a headlock.

Tommy protested, laughing, and Liam let him go.

Aidan pulled him aside. "You mind if I duck out for an hour or two? We're only a half hour from Basking Ridge, and Ellen can meet me at a Starbucks halfway."

"Can't keep you from seeing your cousin," Liam said. "Not when you've been so good about my family. Tell Ellen I said hello."

"You're sure it's okay to leave you here on your own?"

"Aidan. We took on a bunch of Iranian terrorists, among other sordid people. I can handle my family for a few hours."

At the end of the afternoon, after most people had left,

he found himself in the living room with his mother. "I'm glad we talk to each other," she said. "Mrs. Demian down the street talks to her son once a year but hasn't seen him in person in years. Her daughter belongs to some kind of cult in Florida. And Sister Clare at the church? Her whole family was killed in Northern Ireland years ago."

"You've got Frannie and Jeannie," Liam said. "And I promise I won't wait another ten years to come back."

"That would be nice," she said. "I haven't got a lot of years left."

"Come on, mom, you're sixty-five. That's like the new fifty."

She laughed. "Maybe it is. But I still like to see my sonny boy in person now and then."

Aidan returned from his meeting with his cousin, and Jeannie and Frannie promised to clean up the kitchen. Liam hugged and kissed them all, even Tommy, and then the three of them went back to the SUV for the drive to Short Hills.

"Are you glad you saw your mother again?" Aidan asked, when they were on the road.

"I am. She's mellowed over the years. There isn't so much anger there anymore. Though don't get her started on politics. I told her that's a reason we live in France."

"I hear her when we talk," Edwin said. "She's lonely, and she listens to the AM radio for company. They've poisoned her mind."

"But knowing you has been good for her," Liam said. "Thank you for that."

"What can I say? She's my blood."

Liam thought about that statement that night when he and Aidan were in bed together. "Did you have a good time with Ellen?"

"I did. We talk on the phone and we email, but it's not the same. There's a kind of connection you only get in person." He turned on his side to face Liam. "Did you feel that today?"

"I did. I've spent so long trying to distance myself from my family, because I felt I was so different from them. But being together, it's easy to remember we're all people. I love the found family we have in France, but it's nice to have the connection to blood kin, too."

Sunday morning they packed up. While Edwin returned the key to Mary Elizabeth's next-door neighbor, Aidan did a quick vacuum and wipe down of the counters. "I know Mary Elizabeth will probably send her maid through to clean up after us, but I don't want her to think we abused her hospitality," he said to Liam.

On the way to the airport, they stopped at a superstore to buy a locked hard-sided container to send the guns through as checked baggage. Then they had to declare them to the gate agent as they checked the bags. The agent checked the brand of container against a list online. "This brand can't be easily opened," she said. "It's good to go through."

It was comforting once they had gone through the TSA check to let his guard down a bit. If anyone was after them, they wouldn't attempt anything at a heavily guarded airport. As soon as they got on the plane, he performed his pre-sleep routine, imagining the heat radiating through his body, and he was out until Aidan reached over and elbowed him.

It was early evening in Fort Lauderdale, the sky a pale blue mottled with pink clouds. The airport was crowded with people arriving for vacations in the sun. "I keep reminding myself how lucky I am to live in a place where people have to work all year to save up for a week's vacation," Edwin said, as they navigated the crowd to the outside, where they hopped on a shuttle bus to the car rental facility.

"We feel the same way about the French Riviera," Aidan said. "Though most of our clients could afford to live anywhere they want."

They rented another SUV to drive back to Boca. "It seems silly, since we're going to fly out tomorrow," Liam said.

"Trust me, it's easier and quicker than taking a cab or an Uber," Edwin said. Aidan drove and Liam sat in the back once more, watching the highway pass by. Drivers seemed even crazier than they had been in New Jersey, low-slung sports cars weaving in and out of traffic, truckers leaning on their air horns, and elderly people driving sedately at 55 in the fast lanes.

He leaned forward. "Is there anyone driving that car in front of us?" he asked.

"Short old person," Edwin said. "You can barely see the top of his head. And that's a Tesla to our right. Must have the self-driving feature on because it looks like the driver is reading a magazine."

"Give me the slow, narrow back roads of Provence," Liam said.

They pulled up at the gatehouse for Boca Largo, and Edwin leaned across Aidan to show his driver's license. The guard raised the arm and they drove through. "Home sweet home," Edwin said as they pulled into the driveway.

"I'm looking forward to saying that tomorrow," Liam said.

They unloaded their packs from the back of the car and

Liam checked the alarm. Still engaged, with no breaches. That was what he liked to see.

"I'm going to do a load of laundry so we have clean clothes back home," Aidan said.

"I'm going for a quick run," Liam said. "Stretch out my muscles."

"And I'm simply going to relax," Edwin said. "It has been a hell of a time."

Liam loped easily down Gentle Rain Drive and began his circuit of the community. He hadn't wanted to take this job, to come to Florida and see a cousin he barely remembered. But the visit had changed him, or at least his attitude toward his family. How that would play out in the long run he had yet to see.

At least Edwin was going to be safe, and he and Aidan would be back home, together. That was what mattered in the end.

When he got back to the house, he found Aidan and Edwin in the living room, sharing a book. "This is Darius's diary," Aidan said, holding it up. It didn't look like a diary, with its torn paper cover.

"It's beautiful," Edwin said with wonder. "Darius didn't want to show it to me, and I didn't pry, but I'm glad that Aidan brought it out."

"There's a drawing toward the end," Aidan said. He held the book out to Liam. "Look at how he drew Edwin."

The man on the page was much younger, closer to the Edwin that Liam remembered. Edwin claimed he was drab and probably dressed in bright clothes because of that, but the man Darius had drawn was handsome. Shading emphasized the planes of his face, and the hint of a smile predicted there was a sense of humor inside.

"This man is not dull," Liam said, after he'd analyzed it.

"He's full of life. And I can sense the love that Darius put into this drawing. Compare it to these others, the sketches of his dresses. He spent a lot of time on this."

Edwin's eyes were damp. "He loved me," he said. "Sometimes I didn't know why, when he was so handsome and full of life, and I thought of myself as a boring prep school graduate from the rich suburbs of New Jersey. But he saw something in me."

"That's still there," Aidan said, putting his hand over Edwin's. "You'll see it again eventually."

That evening they prepared for bed for the last time in Edwin's house. "You're so good with people," Liam said. "I see it all the time. Even when you're buying a cup of coffee, you have a genuine interaction with the person across from you. I admire the way you've handled Edwin during this trip. You've never belittled Darius or tried to shy away from Edwin's grief." He smiled. "And I see the way you handle me, too."

"I don't consider it handling," Aidan said. "One of the things I learned as a teacher was that you have to figure out what the student needs, and then provide it. Back in the day, sometimes it was more than language lessons. They needed to feel reassured that they could survive in a new country. Advice about the simplest transactions. Courage to face every day."

"And what do I need?"

"We need each other," Aidan said. "Full stop."

Acknowledgments

Thank you to the usual suspects. Randall Klein provided excellent editorial advice and Kelly Nichols developed a killer cover. Joanna Campbell Slan is a great sounding board. My beta readers Andy Jackson, Tim Brehme and Judith Levitsky took time out of their lives to help me make this book better for readers. All remaining errors are my own fault, though!

I couldn't keep writing these books without the love and support of my husband, Marc, and the affection of our wonderful golden retrievers, Brody and Griffin.

www.ingramcontent.com/pod-product-compliance
Lightning Source LLC
LaVergne TN
LVHW012014060526
838201LV00061B/4303